PONNIYIN SELVAN BOOK 5

DEATHLY SWORD

KALKI

TRANSLATED BY NANDINI KRISHNAN

ekadā

ekadā

First published in Tamil as *Ponniyin Selvan*

Published in English in 2025 by Ekadā, an imprint of Westland Books, a division of Nasadiya Technologies Private Limited

No. 269/2B, First Floor, 'Irai Arul', Vimalraj Street, Nethaji Nagar, Alapakkam Main Road, Maduravoyal, Chennai 600095

Westland, the Westland logo, Ekadā and the Ekadā logo are the trademarks of Nasadiya Technologies Private Limited, or its affiliates.

ISBN: 9789360451189

10 9 8 7 6 5 4 3 2 1

This is a work of fiction. Names, characters, organisations, places, events and incidents are either products of the author's imagination or used fictitiously.

Typeset by Jojy Philip

Printed at Thomson Press (India) Ltd

DEATHLY SWORD

'Kalki' is the pen name of Ramaswamy Krishnamurthy (1899–1954), whose career in writing and journalism began as activism during the struggle for Indian independence. He served as editor of the popular Tamil magazine *Ananda Vikatan* before launching *Kalki*. The magazine—and eventually its founder—was named for the mythological tenth avatar of Vishnu to symbolise a vision to 'destroy regressive regimes, express radical thoughts, take readers into new directions, and create a new era'. Kalki wrote several novels, including *Parthiban Kanavu* and *Sivakamiyin Sabadam*, as well as political essays, film reviews, dance and music critiques and scholarly work.

Nandini Krishnan is the author of *Hitched: The Modern Woman and Arranged Marriage* and *Invisible Men: Inside India's Transmasculine Networks*. She has translated two of Perumal Murugan's works into English: *Estuary* and *Four Strokes of Luck*. She was shortlisted for the PEN Presents translation prize 2022 and the Ali Jawad Zaidi Memorial Prize for translation from Urdu 2022. She is an alumna of the Writer's Bloc playwrights' workshop by the Royal Court Theatre, London. Her novel-in-manuscript was a winner of the Caravan Writers of India Festival contest and showcased at the Writers of the World Festival, Paris, 2014.

CONTENTS

1

KODIKKARAI

The storm tore its way through the sea to the shores of Chozha Naadu and then entered the kingdom. Everywhere it went, it left devastation in its wake, as if to illustrate the saying, *Kallulimangan pona vazhi, kaadumalaiyellaam thavidu podi*—where the Kallulimangan[1] goes, forests and mountains disintegrate into powder.

All the way from Kodikkarai to Kaveri Poompattinam[2], one could see evidence of the terrible dance Vayu Bhagavan had staged. Uprooted trees lay on their backs, shorn of their branches. The winds had carried the roofs of houses to faraway places and thrown them violently to the ground. Huts had been reduced to little walls of mud.

In Kodikkarai, it was as if the land had turned to water, as if the sea had swallowed the earth whole. And yet, the white sands proved this notion false. Upon these white sands were patches of stagnant water. These pools hid pits of quicksand. If man or beast were to step into one of these puddles, the unfortunate being would be buried alive. The storm had now empowered these pits to feast on elephants and burp their satisfaction.

Two days after the storm hit the shore, Periya Pazhuvettaraiyar arrived at Kodikkarai, along with his entourage. The Pazhuvoor Ilaiya Rani's palanquin followed. This time, though, its occupant was indeed Nandini Devi.

When she had argued that there was no longer any reason for Madurantakar to travel in secret, and besides—just in case there were to be cause for discretion—it would be useful to have the palanquin at the ready, her husband had been only too happy to acquiesce. Overcome as he was with desire, he barely needed an excuse to keep his ethereal wife by his side.

They had preceded the cyclone to Nagapattinam. Here, the Dhanadhikari saw to his official duties. Back in the day, Nagapattinam was among the busiest ports of Tamizhagam. Goods from foreign lands arrived at its shores on gigantic vessels, from which they were ferried to land by thousands of boats, which would then deliver the goods received in barter to those very vessels. Officials had been appointed to ensure that the customs duty was collected. And it was the Dhanadhikari's right and responsibility to supervise these officials and ensure that everything was above board.

Once he had fulfilled the obligations of his job, Periya Pazhuvettaraiyar visited the famous Choodamani Buddhist Vihara in the city. The monks received him with the grace and respect owed to his rank. He asked them whether they lacked for anything, and whether their place of worship needed something. The monks assured him they had all they needed thanks to the emperor and asked him to convey their gratitude to Sundara Chozhar.

We must now apprise our readers of an incident that had preceded Periya Pazhuvettaraiyar's visit.

Some days earlier, two monks from this vihara had gone to Thanjavur to meet Sundara Chozhar. They had said the entire Buddha Sangam was praying for the emperor to get well. They also had high praise for the service Prince Arulmozhi Varmar had rendered the religion in Lanka, by commissioning the renovation and rebuilding of dilapidated viharas. This initiative had delighted the sangams in Lanka, they had said.

'Chakravarti Perumane[3]! We have another delightful bit of news for you. We've heard that most of the sangams in Lanka are in favour of crowning your younger son the emperor of Lanka! They have been discussing it intently among themselves, and hope to see him ascend to that ancient throne. Could there be any greater honour for our prince?' the monks had said.

Periya Pazhuvettaraiyar had been present at this meeting, and these words had given him a brainwave.

Once the monks had left, the Dhanadhikari addressed the emperor. 'Lord of the three worlds! Your authority holds firm in every one of the eight directions. There is no one in this whole wide world who is not bound to obey your command. However, your two sons seem to have exempted themselves from this. Aditya Karikalar refused to obey your wish that he come here and sends a scroll inviting you to Kanchi instead. The person who is influencing his mind into such twisted thinking is none other than your father-in-law, Tirukkovaloor Malayaman. As for your younger son in Lanka, you've asked him to come back here several times. I'm tired of sending messengers out to him. Kodumbalur Periya Velaan sits there, preventing our men from meeting the prince. So, the scrolls we send don't reach him either. That can be the only explanation, for your youngest child would never disobey you. With things standing as they are, an idea just occurred to me. If I have your permission, I'll give voice to it.'

Once the emperor granted him permission, Periya Pazhuvettaraiyar said, 'Let us charge the prince with the crime of conspiring to crown himself the king of Lanka and order his arrest. Boothi Vikrama Kesari cannot stand in the way of such a command. And even if he tries to do that, as long as we find a way to convey to the prince that this is *your* order, he will certainly come here at once.'

Sundara Chozhar smiled. It was certainly a bizarre plan. But why not give it a shot? He was aching for a glimpse of his Ponniyin Selvan. He sensed that death was at his door, and wanted to speak to his beloved son about his thoughts on the succession to the throne. If Arulmozhi Varman knew that his father wished to hand over the Thanjavur crown to Madurantakar, he would not object. It would be a fairly simple task to persuade Aditya Karikalan to come round to this view, with Ponniyin Selvan's help.

And so, the emperor had agreed to the plan Periya Pazhuvettaiyar had proposed. An order from the emperor was duly sent, for the arrest of Arulmozhi Varmar in the name of Sundara Chozhar. The captain of the ship was also charged with ensuring that not a hair on the prince's head be harmed.

Once two warships had departed for Lanka to fulfil this command, Periya Pazhuvettaraiyar felt unsettled. He was all too aware that if anything untoward were to happen to the prince, the blame would be placed squarely on him. And so, he decided to leave for Nagapattinam, where he intended to receive the prince and then personally escort him to Thanjavur.

There were other motivating factors for this plan too. He had to make sure the prince did not meet Sembiyan Mahadevi or Princess Kundavai on his way to Thanjavur. The two women exerted a tremendous influence on the prince. And both despised Pazhuvettariyar. They were quite capable of meddling with the prince's mind and messing things up before the big day—the death of the emperor.

To top it all off, ever since the guard in charge of the secret passage had been assaulted from behind, the Dhanadhikari had been battling a series of troubling suspicions. Who had attacked the guard? Could someone have been hiding in the subterranean treasure trove? If so, who could it have been? Perhaps the scion of the Vaanar clan, who had evaded capture by his brother's men? In that case, how many secrets he must have learned, hearing and seeing all that he might have!

Even worse, could it be as Chinna Pazhuvettaraiyar had said? Could it be that the mantravadi who came to visit Nandini ever so often had something to do with it all? He would have to find out.

When he had found out that it was Kundavai Devi who had sent a scroll to Prince Arulmozhi Varmar through Vandiyadevan, Periya Pazhuvettaraiyar had panicked. What could she have written? Perhaps that she-snake knew that the Dhanadhikari had been among the conspirators at the Kadambur palace? Could she have mentioned that in the scroll?

Whatever the case might be, it would be most prudent that he receive the prince. He had also ordered that Vandiyadevan be arrested along with the prince. And so, it was crucial that Periya Pazhuvettaraiyar met them at the very shore. He had to ascertain for himself how much Vandiyadevan knew about what.

So, it was that the ageing warrior made for Nagapattinam.

Nandini Devi had even more reason to be there. She was keen to meet Vandiyadevan again and learn what message Kundavai Devi had had for Arulmozhi Varmar. She couldn't wait to find out how successful Ravidasan's mission had been, either. And this was why she had insisted on accompanying her husband to Nagapattinam. Not that the latter had needed much persuasion. He had a vision of Nandini and himself sailing on the seas, as the breeze hit their faces and the colours of the sunset added romantic shades to the evening. Perhaps their marriage would finally be consummated on this trip, the old man thought.

And that was the reason for their voyage to Nagapattinam. We can now bring our readers back to the present.

As it happened, the couple had arrived right in time for a vantage view of the storm. Nandini enjoyed every bit of the havoc it wreaked on the port. She laughed as she saw the waves rise to the height of coconut trees. However, her husband found his hopes of romantic boat rides dashed.

Once the storm had torn its way through the coast, Periya Pazhuvettaraiyar went to take stock of the damage it had caused. He learnt that most vessels had either refrained from going out to sea or had returned, since they had been forewarned about the cyclone. However, the fishermen who had been out during the storm told him that two ships had been caught in the thick of it while journeying from Eezham to Tamizhagam, and that one had caught fire and sunk.

This was cause for grave anxiety. The two ships could well have been the ones he had sent to apprehend the prince, Periya Pazhuvettaraiyar thought. What had become of Arulmozhi Varmar? If he had come to the slightest harm, the entire kingdom would place great blame on Periya Pazhuvettaraiyar. The prince was the object of the unstinted adoration of the subjects. What explanation could Periya Pazhuvettaraiyar offer the people? Or the emperor?

He had to find out what exactly had happened. It would be best to head for Kodikkarai. Anyone who might have actually witnessed the incident was most likely to be there, as were survivors—if any—from the ships. Yes, he would leave for Kodikkarai right away, he thought.

Nandini seemed all too happy to acquiesce when he made the suggestion. 'I've never seen Kodikkarai before,' she said. 'I've heard it's a quite beautiful place. Here's an opportunity to finally go there.'

There were two routes to Kodikkarai from Nagapattinam—through the road and through a canal. Given the size of Periya Pazhuvettaraiyar's entourage, it made most sense to travel by road. Besides, Nandini preferred this option, partly because she was scared a sea voyage would fan the flames of her husband's unrequited lust and partly because going by road would give them the opportunity to meet and interrogate the boatmen and catamaran plyers who had survived the storm and might have news of the ships' and prince's fate.

These interviews didn't contribute much to their knowledge of what had happened at sea. Some of them confirmed that a ship had indeed caught fire and sunk, and claimed to have witnessed it themselves.

When they reached Kodikkarai, the lighthouse keeper—Poonguzhali's father, as we know—rushed out to meet them and offered his humble abode to the couple for their stay. There were no palaces or mansions that they could use in this little coastal town. Even so, Nandini turned down the offer. She wanted them to set up camp close to the lighthouse instead.

The men got busy setting up tents for the couple and their entourage. As if on cue, a ship appeared on the horizon the moment they finished. It came as close to shore as it could, and then dropped anchor.

He had no sooner seen it than Pazhuvettaraiyar's apprehensions doubled and redoubled. The sails of the ship were in tatters. Clearly, it had been caught in the storm. Who might be on board, he wondered. Could the prince be on the ship? The tiger flag had not been raised, but that had little significance—the flag would have been torn to shreds by the winds. Periya Pazhuvettariyar sent a boat out to make enquiries. The men on the ship seemed to have been waiting for a boat. When it arrived, two of them jumped onto it. One was Parthibendra Pallavan.

Since the prince hadn't returned from his mission to save Vandiyadevan, the Pallava scion was frantic with worry. As soon as the winds had abated and dawn had broken, he had scoured the seas for the prince. He finally found one of the men who had accompanied the prince, barely alive. When the man was able to speak, he told them of the fate that had befallen the ship, with both the prince and Vandiyadevan on board. Parthibendran was shattered. A tiny part of his mind told him that there was a chance they had swum to safety. He nursed the mildest hope that the prince might have reached Kodikkarai. This had propelled him on to the very shore where the Dhanadhikari was camped.

When he learned that Periya Pazhuvettaraiyar and his wife were awaiting him, Parthibendran could barely contain his fury. He remembered every word his friend Aditya Karikalan had spoken about the Pazhuvoor Ilaiya Rani. He couldn't help feeling curious about the woman who had stolen his friend's heart and driven the crown prince mad. Curiosity slowly overtook his rage at her for breaking Aditya Karikalar's heart, and he suddenly found himself desperate to meet her. But what if he didn't get the chance? Pazhuvettaraiyar was notorious for hiding his wife away from other eyes. He was beside himself with anxiety now.

This anxiety didn't last long. He was escorted straight to Periya Pazhuvettaraiyar's tent. Standing at the entrance was the Dhanadhikari, his mighty frame in a regal stance. What a mistake it had been to dismiss him as an 'old man', Parthibendran thought now. His physique belied his age. Indeed, he was fitter of body and mind than many a younger man, the Pallava scion thought. A lion of a man.

Even as these thoughts were running through his head, a woman emerged from the tent. It hit him like a bolt of lightning shooting through the dark skies. The woman was light itself. One simply couldn't tear one's eyes away from that exquisite face.

To see her standing before Pazhuvettaraiyar was to see a delicate creeper blossom before an ancient, gnarled tree. Parthibendran, who was already stupefied by her appearance, saw her raise her piercing eyes to his face and heard her say, 'Nadha! Who is this young warrior? I don't think I've ever seen him.' Her voice was as nectar poured from a golden cup. Parthibendran was intoxicated as he had never before been.

2

A WEB OF DESIRE

No old man who marries a young woman is exempt from feeling a gnawing suspicion towards all strangers. In the world of doubt and anxiety from which they have no escape, it is but natural for them to feel irritated by any younger man. Pazhuvettaraiyar had reason for more irritation than usual. He didn't like it one bit when Nandini stood before him and spoke directly to other men. But he couldn't bring himself to snub her either.

And so, he decided to drop a hint. 'Rani!' he said, before Parthibendran could respond, 'The world is very large, and there are millions of people whom we don't know. We can't know every one of them, surely! And it is no great loss either.'

Parthibendran said, at once, 'Aiya! It is no loss in the slightest for the queen consort of this beloved king of Pazhuvoor not to know who I am. The loss is entirely mine. And so, please permit me to introduce myself. Ammani! They call me Parthibendra Pallavan.'

'Oh! Is that so? Why, then, I have heard your name!' Nandini said.

'Parthibendra! Why would you introduce yourself with just your name, leaving out all the honours and epithets to which you're entitled? Nandini! He is not just Parthibendran. He is Vengiyum Kalingamum Vendru Veerapandiyan Thalaikkonda Parthibendra Pallavan—Parthibendra Pallavan, Conqueror of Vengi and Kalinga and Beheader of Veerapandiyan!' Pazhuvettaraiyar said, in a voice dripping with sarcasm.

For a moment, Nandini's face was as a dark cloud in a stormy sky. Two bolts of lightning shot from her eyes and disappeared at once.

The next moment, she laughed.

'Aiya! How many men lay claim to this title, Beheader of Veerapandiyan? Is anyone keeping count?' she asked.

'Ammani! The Dhanadhikari is being all too generous to me. To tell you the truth, I cannot lay claim to that title. Aditya Karikalar is the lone claimant to the honour of having beheaded Veerapandiyan.'

'Why are you being so dismissive, son? Don't you want any part in the glory of having trampled on a dead snake?' Pazhuvettaraiyar said mockingly, and snorted with laughter.

'No, arase, no! Aditya Karikalar did not kill a dead snake! When he raised his sword, Veerapandiyan was very much a living snake. A woman as beautiful as Mohini from Devaloka stood between them. She went down on her knees and pleaded with Aditya Karikalar to spare Veerapandiyan's life. If I'd been in his place, I'd have flung my sword to one side. Veerapandiyan would have lived,' Parthibendran said, his eyes fixed on Nandini although he was addressing her husband.

Nandini, aware that the conversation was taking a dangerous turn, smiled at Periya Pazhuvettaraiyar. 'Nadha, why are we wasting our time on these old stories now? We haven't asked our guest on what mission he has made the journey here.'

At once, Pazhuvettaraiyar said, 'Yes, thambi, why are we retelling the same old tale? Tell us *your* tale, now. Why have you laid anchor here?'

Parthibendran, who had lost possession of his senses after having laid eyes on Nandini, now remembered why he was here.

'Aiya! Do forgive me. I've gone on and on, without telling you the crucial news I bring. I have terrible news, news that would sink all of Chozha Naadu into an ocean of sorrow. Prince Arulmozhi Varmar, who boarded this ship with me at Eezham, jumped off the deck during the storm at sea. We have no idea what became of him. I came here to see if he had made it to this shore. I was hoping I would find him alive and well.'

Before he could finish his speech, Pazhuvettaraiyar hollered, 'What! What are you saying!'

As he spoke, he fell to the ground, as a giant tree that had been uprooted by the cyclone.

Parthibendran leapt forward to lift him up, but Nandini blocked his path and gripped the hand he had extended. Shoving Parthibendran's arm aside, she sank down to the ground by her husband's side, cradled his head with her delicate hands and laid him gently on her lap.

'Water!' she called. 'Someone bring me water!'

A servant ran forward with water. Several soldiers came running too, as did the keeper of the lighthouse, along with his family.

Nandini commanded them, in an authoritative tone, to stand aside. She sprinkled some water on Periya Pazhuvettaraiyar's face.

'Nadha!' she cooed to him softly. 'Nadha ...'

The old man came to, within a few minutes. And then he remembered what he had heard.

'Nandini! Did I dream it all? Did I really hear what I did? What did this Pallavan say? He said the sea had swallowed Ponniyin Selvan, didn't he? When that strapping young man was a toddling boy, I have hoisted him up on my shoulders and delighted in his laugh at our little game. And it was with those very hands that once held his small body that I placed the seal on the scroll ordering his arrest. Aiyo! What will Chozha Naadu say about me? How will the people remember me?' Pazhuvettaraiyar cried, and began to bang his head against his enormous hands.

Nandini had never imagined this war hero, hard as diamond and unbreakable as steel, could ever break down and sob like this. No one had ever seen him in such a state.

'Nadha! Don't panic. He hasn't finished what he was saying. Let's hear him out, and then decide the next course of action,' Nandini said.

'Yes, you're right. Parthibendra, make it quick. You said Ponniyin Selvar had drowned in the sea, didn't you? You said he's dead, didn't you? Is that true? Or have you been driven by evil intentions to make up such a heinous story? You're dancing before a starving tiger, you hear? Beware!' Pazhuvettaraiyar said, his eyes blazing.

'Aiya, please forgive me for contradicting you, but I did not say the prince was dead. I cannot believe that Tamizhagam could have incurred such a terrible loss. I only said he jumped off my ship at the height of the tempest. He might have got out alive, by the grace of God. He might have been washed ashore. It was hoping against hope I would find him here that I made my way to Kodikkarai.'

'He jumped off the ship at the height of the tempest, you say! Why? Why did he jump? And why did he board your ship in the first place? What were *you* doing when he jumped?' Pazhuvettaraiyar fired question after question at Parthibendran.

Nandini cut in at this point. 'Aiya, the story must begin from an earlier point. Let him tell us what he was doing in Lanka in the first place.'

'Yes, start at the beginning and tell me everything. Don't you dare lie! If you don't speak the truth, you will not have a chance of escaping from here. I ...' Pazhuvettaraiyar growled at Parthibendran, gnashing his teeth as he spoke.

'Arase! It is not in my nature to speak anything but the truth. Even if I intended to lie, my tongue would not bend to my will. So, hear me out. News reached Kanchi of a conspiracy against Chozha Naadu hatched by you, Kadambur Sambuvarayar and several others.'

'Lies! Lies! All lies!'

'Let the news be false. It is my great hope that it was lies we heard. I hope and pray it was a lie, but this was the news that reached Kanchi. It was after this that Tirukkovalur Malayaman and Aditya Karikalar despatched me to Eezham, with instructions to bring Arulmozhi Varmar back with me.'

Having started his story with this, Parthibendran recounted everything that had happened until the moment he had landed at Kodikkarai.

Once he was done, Pazhuvettaraiyar cried, 'Kadavule! A terrible thing has happened to Chozha Naadu. And it has happened because of me. I am the paavi who has wrought this ill. It was I who ordered the prince's arrest. It was I who sent those two ships!'

'Arase! You have no part in this. Whether you had ordered the prince's arrest or not, he would have still boarded this man's ship and journeyed to Kanchi, isn't it? Why are you blaming yourself? There is such a thing as destiny that governs the future, that overrules the plans we make. Besides ...' and Nandini whispered something into her husband's ear. At this, Pazhuvettaraiyar's face brightened slightly.

'Yes ... yes, of course ... this didn't even occur to me!' he said. Then, he turned to Parthibendran and said, 'Pallava! I'm going to search your ship. You must stay right here until I return. If you so much as think to run, my soldiers will impale you with their spears. Make sure you don't die with a spear in your back, you come from a family of heroes.'

'Vandanam, aiya! I have no intention of escaping. And if I did have this intention, all your soldiers together wouldn't be able to stop me. I don't plan to take a spear in my back either,' the Pallava scion said.

'Arase! You need not worry on his account. I'll keep watch over him myself. If he tries to run, this knife will pierce his chest at once,' Nandini said, pulling out a pen knife from her waistband. 'Set your mind at rest and go on, search the ship. Interrogate the sailors too, and make sure this man has spoken the truth.'

'Rani! Why must *you* take on the responsibility of staying guard? We have all our soldiers to do this for us. You go into the tent, or to the lighthouse keeper's house. I can even take Parthibendran along with me to the ship.'

'No, I'm not coming, aiya. Your doubts will only be aroused further by my accompanying you. You might think the sailors are validating my account from fear of me. No, I'm staying rooted to this spot. You need not worry,' Parthibendran said.

'Nadha! I will be right here until you return. My eyes will be on you throughout, even as I stand here,' Nandini said. Then, she said into her husband's ear, 'Who can tell why he is here? For all we know, he might have come to do some investigating of his own. Besides, no one should get a whiff of the news about the prince until you return from the ship.'

Pazhuvettaraiyar nodded, and got on the boat that would row him to the ship.

Nandini stared at the boat for some distance. Even as she kept her eyes trained on her husband, she was aware that Parthibendran was staring at her, unblinking. All of a sudden, she swung round and looked straight at him. She had expected that he would be embarrassed into turning his face away. But does the honeybee ever shy away from a flower in full bloom?

Nandini held up the pen knife and said, 'Beware! Don't even think of escape!'

'Devi! Why take the trouble to scare me with that knife? Escape, indeed! How would a fish trapped in a net possibly escape? Having been caught in the net you've cast ...'

'What are you saying, aiya? Are you calling me a fisherwoman, who belongs to the Valaignar community? If the King of Pazhuvoor were to hear these words ...'

'I'm not worried about that, Devi! But I'm not referring to fishing nets when I speak of you. I'm referring to the net cast by your piercing eyes, the web you spin, the desire you stir in ...'

'Chhi, chhi! How dare you! I wouldn't even mind so much if you called me a fisherwoman from the Valaignar community. But to speak of me as a harlot who spins webs of desire to trap men! How dare you!'

'I would never say such an ugly thing. Do you have to take the trouble to spin a web? Does a spider weave a web in order to trap flies? It simply builds a home for itself, and flies find themselves drawn to it ...'

'So, now, I'm a spider, am I? Is that how horrendous I appear to you?'

'I can't seem to get anything right. Ah! I should have spoken of you as a lamp, an earthen lamp that glows not so the moth will burn in its flame but to fill the space around itself with light. If the moth is so foolish as to mistake the lamp for a fruit and fall into its flame ...'

'All it takes to put out that lamp is a sudden breeze. Why, a breath of air from one's mouth could blow it out. That's all the power an earthen lamp has.'

'Sure, one can put out a lamp. But who can put out the full moon? The full moon rises not for Samudra Raja, but because Nature has deemed that it must rise at sunset and caress the sky and earth with its cool rays. And yet, look how silly the sea is! How it stirs and bubbles and tumbles and stumbles when it sees the full moon! How it aspires to rise up and reach this fruit that is on too high a branch! How it aches and yearns for something so beautiful and so unattainable!'

'I've heard much about the literary prowess and imaginative powers of Pallava kings. I see that it was no exaggeration now.'

'I didn't quite believe what I'd read in the puranas and epics, until today. I see that it was no exaggeration now.'

'To what do you refer?'

'I've heard that some beings who are empowered to take on the form of a woman have the ability to tuck the entire world and the expanse of the sky beneath their feet. The asuras, having crossed the Sea of Milk for the nectar and even secured the pot, forgot their mission when they set their sights on Mohini. The Sundoba Sundarar brothers, who were once inseparable, started a fight unto death over a woman. The penance of Vishwamitra was ruined by Menaka. Kovalan was caught as a fish in the nets cast by Madhavi. Dasharatha sent his beloved Rama away to the forest to appease Kaikeyi. The entire Roman empire fell to ruin because of one Egyptian queen ...'

'Enough, aiya, enough! Why do you wax poetic on these instances of women ruining entire empires?'

'Don't you see, devi? Do you really not see the analogy I'm making?'

'If you're comparing these women to me, you could not be more mistaken!' Nandini said, switching suddenly from the respectful plural to the familiar singular address.

'There is no mistake. Your power is no less than that of any of those women.'

'You contradict yourself.' With this statement, Nandini switched back to the respectful plural.

'How so, devi?'

'I sent the King of Pazhuvoor to the ship with the intention of speaking to you in private.'

'I understood that, which was why I refused to accompany him.'

'You said a woman tried to save Veerapandiyan and that Aditya Karikalan was unmoved, didn't you?'

'Indeed.'

'Do you know who that woman was?'

'Yes. She is none other than the woman who now lights up the Pazhuvoor palace as the Ilaiya Rani Nandini Devi.'

'If I had the powers you describe, would I not have succeeded in saving the life of the man I sought to protect? Why did I fail to do so?'

'It is true that Aditya Karikalan in his bloodlust was unmoved by your appeal on the day. But I know just how much he has tormented himself in the three years since.'

'How do you know, aiya? Did he tell you himself?'

'He kept it to himself for three years, and it was eating him up from within. I knew that a terrible sorrow was plaguing him, but I didn't know what it was. Just ten days ago, on the eve of my departure for Eezham, he opened up to me. Ever since …'

'Ever since …'

'Ever since, I have ached to set my eyes on the Pazhuvoor Ilaiya Rani.'

'Do you remember, you said sometime ago that if you had been in Aditya Karikalar's place, you would have spared the life of Veerapandiyar?'

'All too well.'

'Did you mean it?'

'I swear I did. You can put me to the test if you are inclined to.'

'Aiya! A doubt nags at me. Should I tell you what it is?'

'Anything you tell me in that golden voice of yours will delight my ears and fill my heart with joy.'

'It strikes me that you speak as you do simply to put *me* to the test. You speak of my spinning a web of desire, but it is you who seek to entrap me with such flattery. You're trying to become my confidant and learn my secrets, read my mind even.'

Parthibendran was startled. It is true that those had been his intentions when he had started the conversation, but he had quite forgotten this during its course. What had started out as an attempt at entrapment had become a plunge into the sea of desire. So infatuated was Parthibendran that he was now ashamed of what he had set out to do, and blurted out, 'Devi! If I ever seek to probe you in order to carry your secrets to someone else, if I even think about spying on you, may lightning strike me dead!'

'Aiyo! Don't say such things!' Nandini cried.

'Why, devi, why?'

'The other man who came from your prince … what's his name …'

'Vandiyadevan?'

'Yes, yes, him. He did his best to pry out whatever information he could from me. It appears lightning *has* struck him dead, as you said.'

'Unfortunately, lightning has not struck him. It has struck the ship he boarded. And what came for his head has ended up landing on Ponniyin Selvar!'

'Poor thing, I feel sorry for Pazhaiyarai Ilaiya Piraatti. The two people she loved most in the world have gone at the very same time. How terrible!'

'Devi, who are the two people of whom you speak?'

'The two people you mentioned. Ilaiya Piraatti has always nursed a special love for her little brother, hasn't she?'

'Yes, the entire world knows that. But the other person who is the object of her love …'

'Why, the messenger your prince sent this way, who else?'

'You mean Vandiyadevan?'

'Yes, indeed.'

'Chhi, chhi! Pazhaiyarai Ilaiya Piraatti, who has the power to direct the future of the entire empire, and that crass, crude, arrogant, conceited, garrulous, presumptuous ... lowly ... that ... that scum ...'

'Yes, indeed, she is quite besotted. That is why she sent him to Lanka with a scroll. It was to ensure he escaped from Pazhuvettaraiyar. Poor thing, this old man believes he is the cause of the prince's misfortune, but it is actually Ilaiya Piraatti who is to blame. If only she hadn't sent that olai ...'

'True, true! None of this would have happened!"

'When my husband returns from the ship, you must explain this to him. If you do, I will be forever indebted to you.'

'Ammani, is this the only way to earn your goodwill? Is there no other assignment you can think of that I can carry out to earn your gratitude?'

'Aiya, there is no shortage of ways in which one might earn the gratitude of a helpless woman.'

'Tell me one or two of those, then. Aditya Karikalar had the opportunity to earn the gratitude you speak of, and he let it slip. And he has been regretting it every moment of every day for the last three years. I will never, ever make that mistake!'

'Do you promise, aiya? Do you really mean that you will do anything a woman says in order to fulfil her wishes?'

'That depends on who the woman is, devi! If you had asked me this question yesterday, I would have told you that nothing would have moved me to go out of my way to fulfil the wishes of any woman I knew. I would have laughed at the very thought. But today ... everything has changed. Try me, why don't you? If I had a hundred lives, I would sacrifice every one of those in the pursuit of the fulfilment of your wishes. If I had a thousand empires under my rule, I would sacrifice them all to bow to your wishes. If you asked me to let go of this world and the afterworld, I would do that without a second thought. If you asked me to forgive my worst enemies and make peace, I would. If you asked me to bring you the heads of my dearest friends and lay them at your feet, I would do that too!'

As Parthibendran blurted out these frenzied words, he trembled from head to toe. His speech was garbled. His lips quivered. His teeth chattered. His hair stood on end. His breath was as the spitting and crackling of the blaze in a blacksmith's furnace.

Readers might be shocked by Parthibendran's change of heart. Why, if someone had told him he would one day speak as he had just done, he would have laughed at them and said that was quite impossible. When he looked back on this day in later years, he would barely be able to believe he had been thus moved.

But this is not something that is unique to Parthibendran. It has to do with human nature itself.

Researchers have dedicated decades of their lives to unravelling the mysteries of the body, only to make little progress. How, then, does one unravel the mysteries of the mind and heart? What drives us to do as we do? What is it that makes us change into the very opposite of all that we have been thus far?

The most brutal of men, whose lives have been a series of sins, suddenly turn into ascetics. They give themselves up to faith, singing the praises of their gods and dancing in the bliss of their devotion, and thus earn the mercy of God. They dedicate themselves to the service of their fellow beings, and one is hard put to believe it was these very men who wrought such acts of cruelty as they did.

On the other hand, the most devout and righteous slip one fine day, and they slip right into the abyss of hell too!

Nandini, having heard out Parthibendran's impassioned speech, now said, 'Enough, aiya, enough! Stop, now. I'm not going to compel you to do any of the terrible things you spoke of. What I'm going to ask of you will bring both of us great joy.'

3

THE HOOT OF THE OWL

Nandini glanced seawards. Pazhuvettaraiyar's boat had neared Parthibendran's ship. She let out a heavy sigh, which hit Parthibendran's heart like a hurricane.

'Devi! Speak to me. Command me. Tell me what it is I must do. There is no need for you to say it will "bring us *both* joy", for there is no separation between your joy and mine. Whatever makes you happy will give me the greatest joy a man could know!' the Pallava scion declared.

Thoughts were raging in his head, accompanied by disturbing images. There was no doubt that this young girl was suffering in domesticity with that wrinkled old man. Why, she was as a caged parrot, waiting to be preyed on by a wildcat. He would have to save this beautiful parrot from her terrible fate. Let her say the word, and he would arrest Pazhuvettaraiyar right away, on this very ship, and cart him off to some land far away where he would throw him in the bowels of a dungeon. What a monster he was! How had he found it in himself to take a woman young enough to be his daughter, even granddaughter, for a wife?

Nandini's eyes were still on the boat and the ship. She watched her husband climb on to the deck.

'Thank god! He has got on board safely. However great a warrior he is, he cannot fight age, can he? I was terrified he would lose his footing while climbing onto the ship.'

Parthibendran felt betrayed. Why was she so concerned about the old man? So what if he slipped off the boat and fell into the sea? His death would be good for the empire, and release her from captivity. So, why did she care whether he lost his footing?

'I understand only now just how much this old man treasures the Chozha clan. Did you see how he broke down at the thought that the prince had succumbed to the sea? Aiya! It is not certain that the prince is dead, is it? There is a chance he might have escaped, isn't there?' Nandini asked.

'No, it is not certain that he is dead. But it is quite impossible for someone to have swum to safety in such a storm. What can we do against destiny, though?' Parthibendran said.

'Destiny is not to blame here. That rakshashi from Pazhaiyarai is to blame! You may not know, aiya, but Kundavai Devi is obsessed with astrology and palmistry. She declared on the basis of her brother's horoscope and the lines on his palm that he would rule the three worlds. Aiyo! The poor thing, how shattered she will be when she learns of that beloved brother's fate! If only I could be by her side to console her through this ...'

Parthibendran could detect an unmistakable note of uncontained joy in Nandini's voice as she spoke these words. For a moment, he was stunned. Then, he decided he must have been mistaken.

'Why must you console her, Rani? It is her avarice that has led to this misfortune. She should suffer for it!'

'How can you say that, aiya? If there is so much as the glimmer of a tear in one of her eyes, ten thousand hearts will break in Chozha Naadu. She is beloved of the people, isn't she? The apple of her father's eyes, his darling daughter who is unsurpassed in beauty in all three worlds!'

'There was a time when I believed it was so ... well, right up until I met you.'

'And what do you believe after having met me?'

'That all of Kundavai Devi's beauty cannot possibly compete with the beauty of your little toe!'

'Of course you say that now. But once you meet her, you'll forget I even exist.'

'Never! Never, ever! Devi! I have told you that you can put me to the test. Command me, right away, what is it you would have me do?'

'I'm in no position to command anyone to do anything. All I can do is request and appeal. Aiya! There is talk that it is only after Pazhuvettaraiyar's marriage to me that fissures have appeared between the men who rule this empire, that there is unrest in Chozha Naadu. I wish to prove that it is not so. That is why I seek your help.'

Parthibendran felt let down. He had expected that Nandini would have some specific wish that he could fulfil, a personal mission on which she would send him. He had been looking forward to returning in triumph, having successfully carried out the task. But she was speaking of political matters now, and it disappointed him.

'Tell me, Rani, what is it that you would like me to do?' he asked.

'Aiya, it is Ilaiya Piraatti who has disturbed the peace of Chozha Naadu. Her highhandedness has upset and angered the suzerain kings and senior officials of Chozha Naadu. She longs to crown her younger brother emperor of Chozha Naadu, one way or another. This was the reason she stood in the way of the squabbling parties reaching a compromise. Now, that reason no longer exists, and we can bring about a compromise. Listen, aiya! Didn't you say that some of the ministers and the high command of Chozha Naadu feel Madhurantakar must be crowned king after Sundara Chozhar? Well, did you know, the emperor has acquiesced too.'

'Is that so, devi?'

'Yes, aiya! Why else would he issue an order for the prince's arrest and deportation from Eezham? Even so, I don't think this is the right solution. There is space for us to reach a compromise, for all parties to leave happy. We could split the empire, couldn't we, so that the region north of the Vellaaru river is given to Aditya Karikalar and the region south of the river to Madhurantakar? Weren't your ancestors, the great Pallavas, content with Thondai Mandalam? Weren't the ancient Chozha kings once happy to rule the little kingdom enclosed by the Vellaaru river?'

'Devi, why are you running all this by me? What does it matter to me who rules the empire? How does it concern me which region belongs to whom?'

'Aiya! I thought you were Aditya Karikalar's bosom friend, that you both trusted each other with your very lives?'

'I've spent all my days earning the trust and aching for the praise and slaving for the well-being of others. I've wasted enough time on all this. From here on out, I will live only for myself! Rani, I've often wondered why I was born, why I'm alive today, how I've escaped every peril I encountered ... perhaps, I thought, I was born to earn back the grand empire over which my ancestors once ruled, to recreate architectural wonders like Mamallapuram, to remind the world of their greatness, their richness of imagination, their courage and bravery on the battlefield, their hunger for territory ... but my heart is not in it. I find no joy in the idea of ruling over an empire or conjuring up a dreamlike city. What did give me joy was serving the

Chozha empire. I felt honoured by Aditya Karikalar's friendship and trust. It is only now that the scales have fallen from my eyes. It is only today that I see why I was born. There! Do you hear the ocean? Do you hear the waves saying, "Yes, yes!" in agreement to my every word? Do you hear the birds flying across the sky saying, "True, true!" to my every statement? Devi! Don't speak to me of empires and their bifurcation. Ask me to sail to the coral island beyond the seas and bring you an armful of priceless coral stones! Ask me to dive into the darkest depths of the ocean and bring you pearls from the very seabed. Ask me to climb the highest peak of the Meru and bring you back the Sanjivini plant! Ask me to fly beyond the skies and fetch the stars, to string them into a necklace and place it around your throat. Ask me to bring you the full moon to serve as a mirror to see your lovely face!'

'Enough, aiya, enough! That Pazhaiyarai Piraatti is already referring to me as a "madwoman". Don't say things that will truly drive me mad!' Nandini said.

Parthibendran felt embarrassed by his outburst now. 'It is not you, but I who has been driven mad. Do forgive me. Tell me what it is you would like me to do,' he said.

'Throughout Chozha Naadu—throughout Tamizhagam, in fact—I have earned a terrible reputation that I want to set right. I seek your help in this mission. I believe people say my wedding to this old man has wrought ruin on the empire. That it was I who instigated Madhurantaka Devar to aspire to the throne, that it was I who convinced the suzerain kings to ally themselves with him. When I die, I don't want this to be the memory people will have of me.'

'Why do you speak of your death? To torment me?'

'Pallava Kumara! Do you know palmistry? Do you believe in it?' Nandini asked, suddenly.

Parthibendran, instead of answering directly, said, 'Why, let me see your hands?'

Nandini extended her right hand. Parthibendran squinted at it and said, 'That's a quite unique set of lines. I'm amazed that I've actually seen such a palm. Let me see the other hand too?'

She held out her left hand. The Pallava scion stared at the palm and asked, 'Devi! Has anyone else looked at these stunning palms of yours and said something about your future?'

'Yes, Pazhaiyarai Ilaiya Piraatti once examined my palms and said ... well ... she said ...'

'What did she say?'

'That I would die young.'

'That's quite right,' Parthibendran said.

'Aiya! Do you see it too?'

'But I can also see that she doesn't know the subject too well. It is true that one of the lines on your palm indicates that you will die young. However, another line negates that by suggesting that you will have a rebirth in this life itself. And once you're reborn, you'll cross the seas and travel to many new lands, many many kingdoms that will give you great joy, and that you will know a life of bliss such that even the most powerful of emperors can only dream of it. And that all this will be wrought by the true, pure, abiding love of a youth you met by chance on a seashore. The lines say that this man will lay down his life to fulfil your slightest whim.'

And even as he said the words, Parthibendran grabbed hold of Nandini's hands and touched his eyes to her palms in a gesture of reverence.

Nandini snatched her hands away and shook them as if to rid them of his touch. 'Chhi, chhi! What did you just do?'

'Please forgive me! I forgot that these were your palms. They looked like twin lotuses blooming before me.'

'If Pazhuvettaraiyar had seen you do this, he would have thrust a spear through your neck!'

'Devi, my only regret would be that I have but one life to sacrifice for you.'

'And you'd waste that one life on such a pointless sacrifice? Rather than hold on to it so you can actually help this orphaned girl?'

'What would you have me do?'

'Chozha Naadu must not go to ruin because of this infighting over inheritance. I need your help for this.'

'What can I do to stop this?'

'If you can convince your dear friend Aditya Karikalar to visit Kadambur Sambuvarayar ... Sambuvarayar has a daughter. If Aditya Karikalar will consent to marriage with her, my wishes will be fulfilled.'

'Why must you plead so much for such a little matter? I'll bring Aditya Karikalar to the Kadambur Sambuvarayar palace. What must I do next?'

'This alliance will end half the enmity. And once the empire is bifurcated so that Aditya Karikalar can rule the northern half and Madhurantakar the southern half, it will end for good.'

'And then?'

'Well, people will stop talking ill of me. And I will then take my fate into my own hands. I will walk out into the middle of the sea, further and further on until I drown.'

'And I will come running after you and save you. We will both be reborn. We will sail to faraway countries that lie across the seas. I will build a grand empire for you.'

'Aiya! Please stop speaking in this vein. I am steeped in the tradition of Tamizhagam, a tradition of chaste wives. I am the dharmapatni of Periya Pazhuvettaraiyar.'

'Devi, tell me the truth ... why did you marry this old man? Do you love him? Or did he force your consent?'

Nandini sighed tiredly. Her eyeballs strayed upwards, and it seemed she was reliving old memories.

'Poor thing, don't blame the old man. I married him of my own free will. I consented with all my heart.'

'Why? What for? What did you see in him that drove you to this decision?'

'I didn't see anything in him. I married him from my desire for the comfort of a royal life, for the luxury of palaces and for the authority my position would carry.'

'I can't bring myself to believe this!'

'Unbelievable, but true. From as far back as I can remember, I was dismissed and bullied and ostracised for being poor, for being an orphan. The girl who targeted me said I did not have the social standing to play with the royal children. It was the unbearable humiliation of those incidents that drove me to this decision.'

'Devi! Who was the girl who humiliated you in this manner?'

'Don't you know? Can't you guess?'

'Ilaiya Piraatti Kundavai, isn't it?'

'Yes.'

'I'll teach her a lesson one day!'

'God himself has punished her. Her beloved brother and cherished lover have perished in one go. I feel sorry for her now.'

'This isn't enough punishment for that arrogant woman!'

'If you fulfil the request I made of you some moments ago, her torment will be complete. Her ambition, to be the hand that moves the sceptre of Chozha Naadu, will turn to ash.'

'I'll fulfil that request. How will you reward me?'

'I will give you whatever you want; ask me for anything that will not go against the traditions of Tamizhagam.'

'Rani, I believe there is a new religion in the lands across the sea. It has spread to Arabia, Baghdad, Persia and other kingdoms. By the laws of this religion, married couples are allowed to separate. There are rituals that will finalise such a separation. After that, even the women are allowed to remarry.'

'Yes, I've heard of this religion myself.'

'Let us journey to one of those lands, and convert to this religion.'

'I daydream of this myself. But do you think it can actually happen?'

'Devi! Whyever not? It can happen, it will happen. Just say the word, and I'll make it happen. I'll set sail with you right away. We'll head to a land far away. By the power of my sword, I will establish a kingdom there. I will seat you on a throne made of gold and studded with the navaratna gems. I will commission a crown so brilliant that those who look towards your face will be blinded by it. I was born for this, for only this. My entire life has been leading up to this. The wars I have fought, the battlefields I have seen, the duels from which I have emerged alive ...'

'Aiya! Look, my husband is on his way back. His boat has nearly reached the shore. Please be silent now. We will discuss these matters later.'

'When, devi?'

'Accompany us to Thanjavur! If not as a guest, come as a captive.'

'Your invitation is all I need,' Parthibendran said.

Pazhuvettaraiyar's boat reached the shore, and the old man got down. He walked towards them, his bearing so heavy with authority it was as if pride had personified itself in his form.

Nandini and Parthibendran stood up to receive him. Pazhuvettaraiyar glared at them. The thought of the two of them talking alone all this while enraged him. He had no outlet for this rage. And so, he internalised the anger. His heart brimmed with hate.

'Naadha! Did you examine the ship thoroughly? Did you interrogate the sailors? Is everything he says indeed true?' Nandini asked, in a lilting voice filled with affection and concern.

Somewhat placated by the sweet notes of his wife's voice, the king of Pazhuvoor replied, 'Yes, Rani. It appears he does speak the truth. The beloved son of Chozha Naadu, the answer to the people's prayers, the scion of the clan, the dearest of Tamizhagam's children, our prince ... he is gone!' He then turned to Parthibendran and roared, 'And none other is to blame for it than this accursed, murderous, evil monster!'

'Aiya! I am not to blame for this, so don't accuse me! The reason for the prince being swallowed by the sea is the demon in female form who controls Chozha Naadu, the Mohini Pisaasu!' Parthibendran said.

At this, the old man's anger knew no bounds. He assumed Parthibendran was referring to Nandini.

'Ada paavi! How dare you!' he cried, and reached for a spear lying on the ground. He hoisted it into the air and aimed it straight at Parthibendran's heart.

Nandini moved quickly and placed her hand on her husband's arm. 'Naadha!' she said. 'What are you doing? How can you smear the weapon that has felled so many enemies with the blood of a guest?'

'Rani! You call this man a guest? Didn't you hear what he said about you?' the old man said, spluttering with fury.

'About me? You think he said that about me? Ask him if I was the woman to whom he was referring. In that case, I will exact revenge myself with my dagger. I won't trouble you to act on my behalf,' Nandini said.

'Aiya! Do I seem like a madman to you? Would I use such words against the Pazhuvoor Ilaiya Rani? I meant the Mohini Pisaasu in Pazhaiyarai. It was Ilaiya Piraatti Kundavai Devi who sent the prince an olai through Vandiyadevan. And it was to save that impulsive fool that the prince dove into the sea, against my pleas. That is why I said Kundavai was to blame for Ponniyin Selvar's death!'

Pazhuvettaraiyar was embarrassed by his impetuous reaction. He did his best to hide it, and snapped, 'Enough! Don't try to pass the blame to anyone else. You do have a big role in the prince's untimely death. How did you allow him to get off the ship in the middle of such a terrible tempest? Now, get lost! Get away from my sight!'

Nandini interjected with, 'Naadha! Don't you think it would be prudent to take him along with us to Thanjavur? Isn't it best he himself relays what happened to the emperor? If not, the people who are waiting to blame us for everything that ails the empire will add this to the list of our crimes, won't they? Why, they might even accuse us of pushing the prince overboard!'

'Let people say what they want to say! I'm not scared of any such thing. I will tear to shreds the tongue of anyone who mouths these words. But he will be useful for one thing in Thanjavur ... Parthibendra! Why are you looking this way and that way? Do you hope to escape from here?' Pazhuvettaraiyar roared, and gestured to his soldiers, who were waiting in attention some distance away. Four of his men came running. 'Tie him up!' he commanded.

The four men approached Parthibendran. The Pallava scion stood still until they were at an arm's distance. And then he showed them what he was made of. Each of the soldiers went flying in a different direction.

'Aiya! If I must be tied up and dragged to Thanjavur, please do not delegate the duty. I'm quite willing to be bound by ropes as long as the hand that ties them is that of the hero of thirty-six battles and bearer of sixty-four scars, Periya Pazhuvettaraiyar! I will not let anyone else get within sniffing distance of me!'

Pazhuvettaraiyar couldn't help breaking into a smile. 'There is little doubt that you were born into the Veera Pallava clan. Tell me whether you consent to accompanying us to Thanjavur. I will take your word for it, and see no reason to bind you with ropes.'

'It is my own wish, in fact, to relay to the emperor myself what happened and how. It would not be fair for the blame to fall on me, would it?' Parthibendran said.

'In that case, let us leave at once,' Periya Pazhuvettaraiyar said.

Right then, the hoot of an owl sounded from the forest some distance from the camp.

Nandini glanced in the direction from which the hoot had come. The others didn't notice the change the sound had triggered in her countenance.

'What a strange forest Kodikkarai has! A forest where owls hoot by day!' Parthibendran said.

They heard two more hoots, identical to the first.

Nandini turned to her husband and said, 'Must we leave right away? Perhaps we can postpone our departure by a day? What if the prince has managed to swim to safety, or hold on to a log and been washed ashore? He could be lying, exhausted, on the sands of Kodikkarai. Or, he might arrive yet.'

'Parthibendra! Do you see how astute the Ilaiya Rani is? This thought didn't occur to either of us, did it? You're right, we should give it another day. And we mustn't simply stay put. We must station men throughout the shoreline to look out for the prince, and also send out search parties.'

'I have no objection, aiya! But I don't believe the prince could possibly have escaped,' Parthibendran said. 'If you had watched the sea swell as I did, you would be quite as bereft of hope as I am.'

But the old man paid him no heed. He stationed his men throughout the shoreline, a kaadham's distance apart. Unable to rest, he roamed the sands all night, his eyes searching the waters for the prince.

4

A WHISPERED EXCHANGE

Poonguzhali's boat swayed as gently as a cradle. It was hard to imagine that just two days earlier, waves the height of coconut trees had raged in this very sea. Now, Ponniyin Selvar and Vandiyadevan were seated in the boat, while Poonguzhali held the oars. But she paddled rather than rowed, as she asked the two men for a detailed account of what had transpired. They answered her questions, and the three were so focused on the conversation that no one seemed in a hurry to get to the shore.

Having exchanged accounts of their adventures during the sea storm, they now turned their discussion to what they must do once they reached Kodikkarai. Vandiyadevan was trying to convince the prince he should head to Pazhaiyarai instead of Thanjavur.

'Your sister wishes to see you at the earliest. The matter is urgent. I've promised her I will escort you there right away. Please, don't make me go back on my word,' he said.

'You ask that I flout my father's orders all for you to be able to keep your word?' the prince asked, irritably.

'The orders were not your father's, were they? They were Pazhuvettaraiyar's,' Vandiyadevan argued. He added, 'And even if you want to ask the Chakravarti about this, which do you think would be better: to meet him of your own free will or as the prisoner of the Pazhuvettaraiyar brothers? Take my word for it, once the news spreads that the brothers had sent out ships to arrest you, the people of Chozha Naadu will be jolted into action. Your motherland will turn into a battlefield. Do you think that would be a good thing? The tempest was a godsend. God himself raised a storm at sea to prevent this empire from descending into chaos. Do you wish to go against the will of God and start a civil war?'

Of all the things Vandiyadevan had said, it was this speech that struck home. The prince knew his friend was right. The land would erupt with people's rage if word got out that the Pazhuvettaraiyar brothers had convinced the emperor to issue orders for Ponniyin Selvan's arrest. He knew just how beloved of the people he was.

After several minutes of silent contemplation, the prince said, 'Even if I were to decide to do as you say, how will I actually succeed? Won't Pazhuvettaraiyar's men be waiting for me in Kodikkarai?'

'This boat-girl will help us out, won't she? How ever many soldiers are waiting for you in Kodikkarai, she can ensure that we slip past them unseen. She will drop us off safely in the forest. Poonguzhali! You hear me? You'll do that, won't you?' Vandiyadevan said.

Poonguzhali was in the seventh heaven of delight at that moment. Her heart was full. Rescuing the prince and sharing space with him on her boat had infused her soul with joy. The thought that she would have to separate from him once they reached Kodikkarai stung her every now and again. If only she could be of use to him in some further way ... what greater blessing could she ask for?

She floated back earthwards at Vandiyadevan's question and replied, 'If we head to the west of Kodikkarai, we'll come to a canal with forest on either side. The vegetation is thick there, and no one can get through it without considerable trouble. We won't be seen.'

'You can drop us off there and then go to Kodikkarai and find out what the word on the street is, no?'

'Yes, I can. There are enough hiding spots where I can stow away the boat while I'm gone.'

'Ilavarase! Did you hear that?' Vandiyadevan asked.

'I did, I did. You're asking me to enter my motherland like a fugitive. To hide like a thief!' the prince said.

Silence reigned on the boat for a while.

Then, the prince asked, 'Samudra Kumari! Why have you stopped rowing altogether?'

Poonguzhali glanced at Vandiyadevan, and then dipped her oars into the water.

'Poor girl, how long will she ply the oars all by herself? Let me help out. Amma, pass me an oar now!' Vandiyadevan said.

The prince smiled at him suddenly, and said, 'My friend! It appears all your plotting is in vain. I'm headed neither to Pazhaiyarai nor to Thanjavur. It appears God has invited me straight to Kailash.'

Vandiyadevan and Poonguzhali looked at the prince in shock. Then, they noticed that his entire body was trembling.

Vandiyadevan hurried to his side and said, 'Aiya! What is this! Your body is shaking!'

'Do you remember the fever that had taken hold of our camp in Lanka? It has got me now. It's not likely I'll survive it,' the prince said. 'Once it strikes, it's very rarely that one recovers.'

His words shook Vandiyadevan like nothing had before. Not even when the ship's sail had caught fire from the lightning had he felt so numb.

The oars slipped from Poonguzhali's hands. Life drained out of her body. Only her eyes, trained on the prince, seemed alive.

The prince's tremors grew more rapid. Soon, his entire body was shaking with spasms.

'Aiya! What should I do? I'm truly lost! Where should we go now? Poonguzhali! There are good physicians in Kodikkarai, aren't there?' Vandiyadevan cried, panicking.

Poonguzhali seemed to have lost her powers of speech.

Suddenly, the prince stood up. He swayed on his feet, hardly able to keep his balance. 'Take me to my sister! Take me to Ilaiya Piraatti right away!' he said, his speech garbled.

Vandiyadevan was thrilled.

But before he could express his joy, the prince cried, 'Akka! I'm coming to see you. Here I come! I won't let anyone stop me now! I'm on my way!'

With that, he stumbled towards the gunwale of the boat, clearly intending to jump overboard.

Thankfully, Vandiyadevan understood that the prince had lost possession of his senses, and caught him before he could climb over the side. However, Arulmozhi Varmar—incredibly strong to begin with—was now fuelled by the fever, and seemed to have gained the might of an elephant. Vandiyadevan realised as the prince struggled against his grip that he could not hold Ponniyin Selvar back without help.

'Poonguzhali! Poonguzhali! Come here, come fast!' he cried.

Poonguzhali jumped out of her stupor and rushed to the prince. She reached out and held one of his arms. The prince looked at her and stopped struggling at once.

When he spoke, his voice was meek and obedient, almost childlike. 'Akka! I won't disobey you. Don't worry, Akka. If it weren't for you, what would have become of me?' With that, he broke into sobs.

He allowed his companions to lead him to the centre of the boat, where they made him lie down. His body was now still, but his eyes darted wildly from side to side. He let loose a string of words that made little sense. His speech came out in a jumble.

Vandiyadevan realised there was no point in consulting the prince about what they should do next. It was his responsibility to save Ponniyin Selvan. Thankfully, this intelligent woman was by his side, as invested in the prince's safety and well-being as he was. And God must be on their side too, or they wouldn't have got out alive through all the trials they had faced thus far.

'Poonguzhali! Row fast, why don't you?' Vandiyadevan said.

Poonguzhali's arms had regained their strength. There was no sign of fatigue now, and the boat sailed swiftly across the water.

Vandiyadevan stood guard by the prince. What if he tried to jump overboard again? He stayed close, so he could stop the prince if he showed any sign of getting up. Even as he kept watch, he knew they had to make a decision now.

'Penne! What do you think? What course of action should we follow? Take our chances in Kodikkarai? Will your family help us out?'

'Aiya! How can one tell who is to be trusted at this time? My brother's wife will do anything for money. My father's salary is paid by the Pazhuvettaraiyar brothers. Besides, the men who are on the lookout for you might still be in Kodikkarai. There is, most likely, a bigger force stationed there, hoping to find the prince,' Poonguzhali said.

Vandiyadevan marvelled at her foresight. What a blessing it was that she was around to help him in this terrible situation!

'So, you agree that it is dangerous to go straight to Kodikkarai?' he asked.

'Look there!' Poonguzhali said.

Vandiyadevan looked in the direction she was pointing. He saw a huge ship anchored close to the shore. The top of the lighthouse peeked at them over its mast.

'Aha! Whose ship could that be? Perhaps Parthibendran's? In that case, isn't it best to take the prince to Kanchi?' he asked.

'It could be the Pazhuvettaraiyars' ship too, aiya! Do you see something beyond the ship?'

'Yes, the lighthouse.'

'And do you find something strange there?'

'No, I can't tell.'

'I can. I can see a crowd of men at the top, their eyes trained towards the sea.'

'Can they see the boat from there?'

'Not until we get closer to the shore.'

'It's best we exercise the utmost caution from here on out. You mentioned a canal to the west of Kodikkarai. Will the boat fit through the canal?'

'Yes, that's our only option. We can get there by nightfall. Aiya! You remember the ruin in the forest, where you hid through the day before we left for Lanka? We can get close to that spot by boat. We can carry the prince to the ruin, and you must keep him company while I go into town and find out what's happening.'

'Does the canal end right there, Poonguzhali? Or does it go further?'

'It goes from Kodikkarai right up to Nagapattinam,' Poonguzhali said.

Ponniyin Selvar was muttering to himself all through. Now, his voice rose and they could hear his words more clearly.

'Yes, Akka, yes! Remember, I told you what the Buddhist monks from Nagapattinam said? Things unfolded exactly as they had predicted. The members of the Maha Sangha offered me the throne of Lanka in Anuradhapura. But I turned them down, Akka! It was because I have no interest in ruling a kingdom. Command me as you will and I'll obey without question—ask of me anything, but this! I have absolutely no interest in ruling an empire ... please don't burden me with that! Do you know, sailing on a boat is so much more pleasant than being king? Listen to me, Akka! There is a boat-girl in Kodikkarai ...'

Poonguzhali all but jumped out of her skin, while Vandiyadevan stared at the prince in shock. They waited with bated breath for what he was going to say next, but he fell silent for some time. And then, it appeared he had regained some measure of consciousness, for he opened his eyes, looked about himself and asked, 'Have we not reached Kodikkarai yet?'

'There, you can see the shore!' Vandiyadevan said.

Before he could decide whether to ask the prince for his opinion, the prince lapsed back into his dreamworld.

His reference to 'the boat-girl' had shaken Poonguzhali. Overcome with a strange mix of embarrassment and shyness, she couldn't bring herself to look either at the prince or Vandiyadevan. So, she kept her eyes fixed on the sea as she rowed towards the canal, manoeuvring the boat towards the south-west.

As she had predicted, they had entered the canal by nightfall. Vandiyadevan saw that the bank on either side was high, and further sealed off from civilisation by trees that grew tall and thick.

Poonguzhali steered the boat to the shore and anchored it there. She whispered, 'Aiya, look after the boat!' and then jumped onto land.

She squirrelled up the tallest tree she could find and took in the view. Then, she hurried back down and said, 'What a mercy we came here! Soldiers have been stationed all through the seashore, a kaadham's distance apart. And an entire assembly is camped by the lighthouse!'

'Could you tell who is camped there?' Vandiyadevan asked eagerly.

'I couldn't see that far, but it must be Pazhuvettaraiyar's men, who else? Whatever it is, let us first make for the place I mentioned. Then I'll head home and find out what exactly is going on.'

'Penne! What if someone catches sight of you? If something were to happen to you, the two of us are done for!' Vandiyadevan said.

'Aiya, I've never thought about my mortality before. I've always treated my life as dispensable, taking risks without precaution. But now, for the first time, I want to guard my life. I must stay alive at least until I get the prince to safety. So, don't worry about me, I won't let anyone get in the way of that,' Poonguzhali said.

She was rowing the boat so gently that the oars barely made a splash. It crawled through the canal. The shadows from the tall trees lining the shore further darkened the water. The stars seemed to be peering anxiously at them from the sky. The reflection of those stars, frequently disturbed by the night breeze, seemed to symbolise the emotional state of the boat's occupants.

After what seemed like an age, but was actually only a naazhigai, Poonguzhali anchored the boat to the shore. She then disappeared through the trees. Well, her body did while her mind and heart remained in the boat. Her soul hovered over the prince, even as she sped through the forest, paying no heed to the thorny undergrowth, the uneven forest floor or to the prospect of encountering wild animals. When the landscape allowed it, she even ran. She was heading for the Kuzhagar temple. She reached the temple gate just as the priest was closing the doors of the sanctum sanctorum. Having made sure no one else was about, she made her way to the priest.

He looked at her in surprise. Although he knew her propensity for making sudden appearances at odd hours, he had been startled by the sight.

'Is it really you, Poonguzhali? I thought it was someone else! There's quite a bustle about town these days. Such commotion and chaos, with all these visitors ... where have you been all these days, Poonguzhali? I was worried about you,' he said.

'I had to go out of town. Swami! I noticed the commotion as soon as I arrived, and that's why I'm here. I wanted to ask you what the matter is,' Poonguzhali said. 'Who are those people stationed along the shore?'

'Do you know nothing at all? Haven't you gone home?'

'I was going homewards, when I saw that an entire camp had been set up nearby. I turned back to ask you who it was. You know I don't like being around strangers.'

'Well, it is Periya Pazhuvettaraiyar who has set up camp there. The Ilaiya Rani is with him too. And, of course, their entourage. The new development is that Parthibendra Pallavan from Kanchipuram has joined them. And he has come with some terrible news. Haven't you heard, Poonguzhali?'

'What terrible news? No, I've heard nothing,' Poonguzhali said.

'Ponniyin Selvar was apparently on board that paavi's ship, when they were hit by a storm at sea. The prince jumped overboard in order to save someone else. And he hasn't been spotted since! Periya Pazhuvettaraiyar's men have been stationed along the shore to see if he happens to make it to Kodikkarai. And the Ilaiya Rani is in such a state! She was here sometime ago, in fact. Poonguzhali, you know people say all sorts of things about her, but they're completely mistaken. She was beside herself with worry for our prince, do you know?'

'Is that so, swami? It warms my heart to hear you speak of the Pazhuvoor Rani's good nature. But why was she at the temple?'

'She came here to pray to Kuzhagar swami, to save the prince somehow. Not everyone can be heartless like you, no? Why, you're entirely unmoved by this news about the prince!'

'What's the point of being moved or unmoved, swami? You yourself have said so often that everything happens as destined. What can we do to fight fate? Well, that's as may be. I don't want to go home while all those grand personages are about. Give me the leftovers from the day's prasadam … you must be carrying it with you. I'll eat that, and then sleep here tonight.'

'You must be the oddest person I've ever met, Poonguzhali! How strange you are! When some grand personage arrives, people usually fall over themselves in order to go make their acquaintance. But you … you can't stand strangers, and you're terrified of important people. What are they going to do, eat you alive? How is being around them scarier than sleeping alone in the middle of the forest?'

'Swami! If you don't want to let go of your precious prasadam, I'll go without it. Don't tell me off for being who I am!'

'Shiva-Shivaa! Where am I telling you off? All I meant was that this meagre amount of prasadam and the hard surfaces of the temple are poor comforts for you … but here, take it all!' the priest said, and handed over the prasadam.

Poonguzhali opened the leaves in which it was wrapped and said, 'You're right, this is barely enough to stave off my hunger. How you stinge over feeding God! Is that fair, now? And what's in that kamandalu? Water?'

'No, the milk that was used for the lord's abhishekam. I'm taking it home for the baby.'

'Well, assume I'm your baby for tonight and give it to me. It will earn you punyam.'

'What a girl you are! Fine, here, take it. But keep the kamandalu safe!'

As the priest, divested of food and milk, was leaving, a loud hoot rent the air.

Poonguzhali asked, startled, 'Aiya! What is that sound?'

'Can't you tell? It's the hoot of an owl. Is there a shortage of owls in the forest of Kodikkarai?' the priest sighed, even as a second hoot sounded.

'Yes, it does sound like an owl!' Poonguzhali said.

'It isn't owls that pose a danger to you, anyway,' the priest said. 'Well, make sure you lock the main gate before you settle down to sleep.'

The moment he disappeared into the forest, Poonguzhali left the temple. She made straight for the spot from which the owl's hoots had come. Her path was interrupted by a narrow water channel. Thazhampoo[1] shrubs grew densely on either side of the channel. Poonguzhali lowered herself into the water, holding on to the shrubs for balance. She ignored the thorns that stung her hands. The blossoming flowers gave off a heady fragrance. Anyone else would have been intoxicated by this fragrance, but Poonguzhali barely noticed it.

She treaded softly, keeping her ears alert for the slightest sound. She managed to filter out the various night sounds of the forest, her ears primed only for ... ah, there it was! Human speech! A whispered exchange between two people, one a man's voice, the other a woman's.

Poonguzhali kept herself hidden as she eavesdropped.

'Mantravadi! Everyone believes, like you, that the prince has died at sea. Pazhuvettaraiyar, too, is a mess of tears. But I don't believe it!' said the woman's voice.

5

RAKKAMMAAL

Once Pazhuvettaraiyar and Parthibendran had left together to patrol the shore, Nandini was alone for a while. She sat contemplatively, watching the waves lap the shore.

'Rani amma!'

Nandini turned upon hearing the voice.

The lighthouse keeper's daughter-in-law stood before her.

'Who are you?' Nandini asked.

'My name is Rakkammaal.'

'What do you want?'

Rakkammaal didn't reply. Instead, she stood staring at Nandini's face.

'What are you staring at? What does my face have that merits such scrutiny?'

'Do forgive me, amma. The moment I saw you, another face came to mind. But ... that cannot possibly be!'

'What are you blathering on about? What cannot be?' Nandini demanded.

'There cannot possibly be any connection between you and that crazy mute woman.'

'Who is the mute woman you speak of?'

'There is a mute woman in Eezham. She's my father-in-law's cousin. His father's elder brother's daughter. She comes here at times too.'

'What does she have to do with me?'

'I told you, didn't I? It's impossible that there could be a connection between the two of you.'

'Then why were you reminded of her when you saw me?'

'My eyes have tricked me. It's just that your face …'

'Resembles hers?'

'It seemed like that at first.'

'Rakkamma! Is that oomai here now?'

'No, amma. She comes here quite rarely. And unannounced.'

'Will you bring her to me the next time she comes?'

'Why, Rani amma?'

'I'd like to meet the woman whose face resembles mine.'

'I told you, my eyes played a trick on me.'

'How can you be so sure?'

'Rani, you belong to Pandiya Naadu, don't you?'

'Yes, and you?'

'I'm from Pandiya Naadu too. But the oomai I mentioned, she's from Chozha Naadu. And hence …'

'That's not important. You're not the first person who has spoken of our mutual resemblance. I'd like to meet her. Will you bring her to me? You will be suitably rewarded.'

'Rani! You might as well have asked me to catch the tempest and bring it to you. She won't stay in one place. And she won't listen to anyone. I told you, she's crazy!'

'All right, all right. Why did you come here now? Will you tell me that, at least?'

'Rani! Two men arrived here a few days ago. They spoke of you.'

'Why?'

'They said they had to make an urgent trip to Lanka at your behest. I convinced my husband to take them there by boat.'

'Has he returned?'

'No. That's why I'm worried. If something has happened to him ...'

'Nothing would have happened to him, don't worry! And if some calamity were to befall him, I will look after you. Do you know anything about his passengers?'

'They have returned. Didn't you hear the owl's hoot a while ago?'

'I did. What of it?'

'Didn't you recognise it? As the mantravadi's voice?'

'How did you recognise it? Do you have some ties with the mantravadi?'

'Yes, Rani!' Rakkammaal said, and made a sign with her hands.

Nandini looked at her in surprise. Then, she asked, 'Where are they now? Do you know?'

'The mantravadi is waiting to meet you.'

'So, why doesn't he come here? Why is he waiting?'

'He does not wish to run into the Pallavan. Apparently, they met in Eezham. He doesn't wish to encounter your husband either.'

'Did you meet the mantravadi?'

'I was drawn by the hoot of the owl. I went to see who it was, and he was there. He asked me to bring you to him. He said he would hide near the Kuzhagar temple. Will you come with me, Rani?'

'How?'

'You can say you're going to the Kuzhagar temple to pray.'

'That's a good idea. But won't I need an escort?'

'No, there's no need. But if you like, we can take Senthan Amudan along.'

'Who is that?'

'My husband's cousin. The son of the mute woman from Thanjavur.'

'Shiva-Shivaa! *Another* mute woman?'

'This family is accursed. Some are mute by birth. Some are mute by nature. And some by order. My husband can speak well enough. It is I who decided he shouldn't.'

'Does the oomai from Lanka have children? Do you know?'

'Apparently, she once gave birth to twins. No one seems to know what became of them. I've been trying to dig up that secret for the longest time, but to no avail.'

'Why has that boy from Thanjavur come here? The son of the other oomai?'

'He came in search of his uncle's daughter Poonguzhali. But she's not here, so he's waiting for her return.'

'Where has she gone?'

'I was about to tell you. The day after my husband took the mantravadi to Lanka, two more men arrived here. And they were being pursued by soldiers from Pazhuvoor. My sister-in-law made off to Lanka with one of them.'

'She knows how to ply a boat?'

'That's all she does with her time. And when she's not in the middle of the sea, she's in the forest. There isn't a nook in the forest she doesn't know.'

'What do you think it means that she hasn't returned yet?'

'These people are going on and on about someone drowning at sea. I say we don't know for certain. Once Poonguzhali returns, we'll know for sure.'

'She could have drowned too, no?'

'No, she won't. The sea is practically her cradle. Besides ...'

'Besides?'

'I was watching from the top of the lighthouse some time ago. I thought I saw a boat in the distance.'

'And then?'

'And then it didn't come to the shore.'

'Where could it have gone, then?'

'They've probably spotted the crowd here and taken it down some hidden canal to avoid us.'

'Is that even possible?'

'There is nothing that Poonguzhali cannot do at sea. Senthan Amudan had accompanied me to the top of the lighthouse. He, too, says he saw the boat.'

'Well, we'll think about all that later. Let's go to the Kuzhagar temple now. Come!'

'Should I call Senthan Amudan along, to escort us?'

'No, let him keep searching for his cousin. I don't want to stand in the way of his mission.'

The two women made for the Kuzhagar temple. Rakkammaal was just as familiar with the forest as Poonguzhali. She led Nandini carefully through the overgrown thickets.

When they arrived at the temple, the priest looked at them in surprise.

'Rani! What is this, you've come here all alone, and at this time of night! Without an entourage! Why didn't you send word? I would have prepared a reception befitting your stature!' the priest said.

'This is no time for such frivolous things! Bhattare[1]! A terrible fate has befallen Chozha Naadu! The prince, who is dearer to the people than their own eyes, has been swallowed by the sea! At least, that's what they say. I would like to pray to Kuzhagar and ask him to save the prince.'

'I'm sure no such thing could have happened. Thaaye! Don't worry. Samudra Raja will not allow any danger to befall our Ponniyin Selvar.'

'How are you so certain, bhattare?'

'The prince's horoscope is such, amma! How can the sea swallow a man who was born to rule the world? Don't worry. Come, pray to Kuzhagar. He will save the prince for sure.'

With that, the priest lit lamps and performed the aradhana for the deity. He then gave Nandini a few spoonfuls of tulsi water.

'Ammani!' he said. 'It gives me such joy to see how you have come up in life!'

'Do you know me from before, bhattare?'

'Yes, Rani. I have seen you in Pazhaiyarai. I have seen you at the temple by the Vaigai shore too. Your brother Tirumalai ... what is he up to these days?'

'He has been going from place to place, singing the praises of the Azhvars. I haven't seen him in a very long time.'

'And that has caused him much distress, amma! He was very upset that you haven't met him since you became the Rani of Pazhuvoor.'

'What can one do about that, aiya? The family into which I have married is one of devout Shaivites. And my brother is a Veeravaishnavan. He's adopted the epithet "Azhvarkadiyaan" and goes about picking fights with devotees of Shiva. How can I invite him to my home? Would it be right to cause my family distress? And can I trust him not to offend them?'

'You're right, thaaye. It is most important to conduct yourself in a way that won't cause your husband any distress. Let Azhvarkadiyaan do what he wants, it isn't your lookout!'

The two women took their leave of the priest.

'Please don't go all alone in this dark. If you will give me just a little time, I'll finish things up here and accompany you.'

'No, aiya, please don't hurry on our account. This woman knows the place well. And the entire town is awake today. Who can sleep a wink until the prince arrives safely? We are in no danger at all. Let us take our leave of you now,' Nandini said.

The two women began to walk away from the temple. As soon as they were out of the priest's sight, Rakkammaal took hold of Nandini's hand and looped around, towards the backyard of the temple. They went past it, and walked on until they saw a canal lined with thazhampoo shrubs. They made their way along the canal's bank, their path lit by the stars.

6

POONGUZHALI'S PANIC

Poonguzhali stood frozen, trying to breathe as quietly as she could and stay well-hidden behind the leaves. Nandini and the mantravadi spoke softly, but she could hear most of their exchange.

When the Pazhuvoor Rani said she wasn't convinced that the prince had drowned, the mantravadi said, 'Rani, you never trust me, whatever I say. But could you tell me, what makes you doubt the truth of this particular news?'

'Haven't you heard of the prince's astounding horoscope? The priest at the Kuzhagar temple mentioned it too.'

'That's insanity! The powers of planets and stars are as nothing to my magical powers. Do you know that it was I who conjured the storm? That spy from Kanchi didn't believe this either, at first. But he must have come around to admitting it even as he drowned to death!'

'Did you see Vandiyadevan drown to death?'

'So what if I didn't? I saw the ship on which he was stranded catch fire.'

'Apparently, the prince jumped into the sea to save him from that burning ship?'

'Did he return?'

'Not to the Pallavan's ship.'

'Then, why are you still in doubt? I left Vandiyadevan alive so I could kill both our enemies at once. He was bait for the prince.'

'I'm not able to believe the two of them are dead. Something tells me they're both still alive. Do you know Poonguzhali?'

'All too well. She was a pain in Lanka, giving us trouble at every turn. In all likelihood, she perished in the tempest too.'

'No, she did not. Some time ago, a boat appeared in the distance. Rakkammaal saw it from the top of the lighthouse. And it disappeared all of a sudden. She thought she saw two or three people in the boat.'

'In that case, leave with that old man right away. I'll keep watch here.'

'Why should I not stay?'

'If the old man stays and finds the prince, he'll give him a royal welcome. All our plans will go to waste.'

'Mantravadi! It strikes me too ... why do they all have to die? As long as everyone consents to crowning Madurantakan emperor ...'

'Ammani! Trust you to reveal your pen buddhi![1] The spy from Kanchi knows all our secrets. He must have told the prince already. Leave before daybreak. Rakkamma! If Poonguzhali has indeed brought those two men here, where would she have hidden them?'

'There's a hidden ruin in the forest. That is her secret den. She kept the spy from Kanchi there through the day before taking him to Lanka. I found out later.'

'Well, good. I know where that ruin is. I'll go await them there. Rani! How is the emperor? Have you had any news?'

'Which emperor do you speak of?'

'This tongue will never bring itself to refer to that invalid Sundara Chozhan[2] as "emperor". I speak of *our* emperor.'

'I had news of him about ten days ago. They say he is well. Aha! How long it has been since we met!'

'All right, all right, leave right away. What does that Pallava moron intend to do?'

'We're taking him to Thanjai with us.'

'Be careful around him.'

'Oh, there's no need to worry about him. He'll lay down his life to fulfil my slightest wish.'

'Even so, it's better to err on the side of caution. You did allow that spy from Kanchi to pull a fast one on you, no?'

'You're right. I did. And that's why I wish to meet him again.'

'Please don't nurse that desire, Rani! You won't meet him alive again.'

With that exchange, they seemed to move away from the spot. Poonguzhali folded herself further into the shadows. Thankfully, they headed off in a different direction and didn't pass by her.

The conversation she had chanced upon had stricken her with panic. Her entire body trembled at the thought of the various dangers that were closing in from all sides on Ponniyin Selvar. He was laid low by a terrible fever. Pazhuvettaraiyar was waiting to arrest him. Conspirators were planning to murder him. And that Mohini Pisaasu in human form was egging them all on. She had even cast her spell on Parthibendran. The hidden ruin, where Poonguzhali had thought the prince would be safe, was no longer a secret spot. Even as her throat constricted and heart beat ever faster and sight grew dim, Poonguzhali's thoughts were all focused on getting back to the boat as fast as she could. The responsibility of saving the prince from all these perils was hers alone. And this was such a heavy burden that she was filled with self-doubt … so much so that, for the first time in her life, she wondered whether she had lost her way in the forest. It seemed to her that she was circling round to the same spot over and over again. What if she ran into one of the prince's enemies now? What explanation could she offer? How was she to escape so that she could save the prince?

No, no, this *was* the right path. There, she could see the canal! Right round the bend was the nook in which she had anchored the boat. Poonguzhali all but flew to the spot.

And then, her heart stopped. The boat was no longer there!

Where could it be?

Could Pazhuvettaraiyar's men have come here in her absence? Perhaps they had arrested the prince and Vandiyadevan? But even that ... even that would be preferable to ... something much worse could have happened! What if Vandiyadevan had carried the prince to the hidden ruin, only to find those murderous men lying in wait? Adada! What a mistake she had made! She had to run to the ruin right away.

She began to tear through the undergrowth, only to wonder for the second time that night, the second time in her life, whether she had lost her way. Perhaps she was just going round in circles.

What was that, now? It sounded like running feet. Behind her! Someone was giving her chase! Who could it be? And why? Was it that awful mantravadi? Well, so what if it was? Why should she be scared of him, anyway? She had a dagger tucked into her waistband. She could take anyone on. There was no need to run.

No! She *had* to run. This was no time for a duel. Her arms were limp from exhaustion. The dagger would not find its mark. She had to escape with her life, because the prince's life depended on her staying alive! Vandiyadevan had warned her earlier, hadn't he? He had said she should be careful, hadn't he? She had promised to be back in one piece. Yes, she would outrun whoever was chasing her. She wouldn't break that promise.

Poonguzhali threw herself into the densest thickets. But her pursuer would not give up. The birds flew away in fright as she launched herself between the trees on which they were roosting. The wild boar, roused from sleep, ran about wondering who was disturbing the quiet of the night. A lone deer came flying from nowhere and rammed into Poonguzhali. For all this, the man chasing her had not given up. She could hear the thundering of his feet, the panting of his breath. Poonguzhali felt drained. She could not run anymore. And then her fatigue turned to rage. How dare this man chase her into exhaustion? She would do him in, whoever he was! Let him come!

7

A SONG IN THE FOREST

Just as Poonguzhali stopped running and turned to face her opponent, a melodious refrain broke through the sounds of the forest, from some spot covered in the darkness of night.

Ponnaar meniyane
Pulitholai araikasaithu
Minnaar senjadaimel
Milir konrai anindavane!

He of the golden skin
Who wears a tiger's skin at his waist
He of the lightning-like locks,
Ornamented with a garland of konrai flowers!

Poonguzhali recognised Senthan Amudan's voice right away. She began to laugh. She forgot that the sound of running feet had been coming from a different direction.

'Aththaan[1]! Is that you?'

'Yes, Poonguzhali!'

'Where are you? Come on out!'

'Here I am!' and Senthan Amudan stood before her.

'You gave me a fright! Why did you chase after me?'

'Poonguzhali, I've made a very long journey from Thanjai, only to see you and hear your beautiful voice. And I've been waiting for days, even after arriving at your home. When I happened to see you, I ran behind to catch up with you. Why did you run away from me? Come on now, sing me a song!'

'What a place to sing a song! And what a time!'

'Well, if you won't sing, I'll sing another song myself. I'll wake all the sleeping animals, and make them run about. Here we go:

Piththaa! Piraisoodi perumale arulaalaa

Madman! You who have worn the crescent moon as ornament
And blessed the Arutturai temple with your presence ...[2]

'That's enough, aththaan! Stop singing now!'

'Will you sing, then?' Senthan Amudan asked beseechingly. Then, he spoke in a quick, low whisper. 'Poonguzhali! Another man was pursuing you. I began to sing loudly to warn you of this, and stall him. He had a secret rendezvous with your brother's wife this evening. Do you know who he might be?' And then, he asked in the same loud voice he had used earlier, 'What do you say? Sing, won't you? Or shall I sing? Why, Lord Shiva dances in sudukaadu! Is it so wrong to sing in an ordinary kaadu?'[3]

'Fine, I'll sing, I'll sing. Don't throw a tantrum now!' Poonguzhali said, and began:

Parakkum em killaikaal! Paadum em poovaikkaal!
Arakkan enaththagum adigal Aroorarai
Marakkakillaamaiyum valaigal nillaamaiyum
Urakkamillamaiyum unarththa valleergale!

Parrots who can fly to him, mynahs who can sing to him!
He, of Aroor, who is the epitome of virtue and justice!
Tell him that I can't stop thinking of him, and so
My bangles slip off, and my eyes stay sleepless![4]

Then, she asked softly, 'Amuda! How did you know I had returned?'

'Poonguzhali! I saw the boat from the top of the lighthouse. I thought it might be you, and so came to the forest to look for you. I saw some of the soldiers from Pazhuvoor come this way too. I found the boat, but you weren't there. My friend Vandiyadevan was. I told him about the soldiers, and the two of us carried the prince to the safety of that old ruin.'

'Aiyo! What a terrible mistake you've made! What became of the boat?'

'We were worried that someone might see the boat, and so we upturned it and hid it in the shallow waters of the pond,' he said in a whisper, and then loudly, 'Why did you stop singing, Poonguzhali! Sing the rest too!'

With this, he began to sing the next refrain.

'Amuda! I wanted to sing the stanza in praise of the Kuzhagar Swami of Kodikkarai, but I've forgotten the lines. Do you remember?'

Kadithaaikkaatru vandetrakkaraimel
Kudidaanayale irundaal kutramo?
Kodiyen kangal kandana kodikkuzhageer
Adigel umakkaar thunaiyaaga irundeere!

On the shore where the wind blows strong
Is it wrong to stay intoxicated?
The eyes of this sinner fell upon the Kuzhagar of Kodikkarai,
He who stood as protector, offering solace to devotees![5]

The moment he stopped singing, Poonguzhali asked urgently, 'Aththaan! Has that man who was pursuing me left now? Or do you think he's hiding somewhere nearby?'

'I haven't heard his footsteps since we came to this spot. He must be hiding somewhere about here. Do you know who he is?'

'All too well,' Poonguzhali said in a loud, cheerful voice. 'How could I not know the song Sundarar sang about the owls of Kodikkarai? That's the one you meant, isn't it? Here it is:

Kaaden migavaal idhu kaarigai anja
Koodi pondhil aandhaigal koogai kuzhara
Vedi thondar saalavum theeyar sazhakkar
Kodi kuzhagavidangoyil kondaaye!

In the dense forest, a frightened woman
Hears the babbling caws of crows, hoots of owls
Yet knows you shield devotees from evil
Your home is the Kodi Kuzhagar temple.[6]

'You see, Amuda? Even back in Sundaramurti's time, owls hooted and crows cawed in this forest, just as they do today. Except, now, we have humans cawing and hooting like those birds too. A while ago, I heard a human owl hoot. Do you have any idea who that evil person might be? Let me see if I can imitate that cry. Here we go! Tell me what you think!'

With that, she screeched just like an owl, thrice in succession.

'You sound exactly like an owl!' Senthan Amudan said. 'I'm used to hearing you sing divine songs in the sweetest notes. Where did you learn this awful screech?'

'Oh, a mantravadi taught me. Apparently, for one's magic to work, one must screech like an owl.'

'You're trained in magic, are you?'

'A little. Do you want to test my powers?'

'How would I do that?'

'I divine with my powers that a man is eavesdropping on us from somewhere nearby. Why don't you search for him, and see whether I'm right?'

Even before she finished speaking, there was a rustling noise among the trees. Ravidasan stepped out of the foliage, laughing loudly.

'Penne! Is this how we're going to play it? I knew you were a master of tantra. Now, you claim to know mantra too, eh?'

'You lowlife! It's you!'

'Penne! Do you know who I am?'

'You're the one who tried to murder the prince in Lanka! But you failed. And so, you raised a sea storm with your powers of magic and made sure the prince and his friend drowned to death!'

'How are you sure they drowned to death? Did you witness it?' Ravidasan asked.

'Their bodies washed ashore when I was in Bhoota Theevu. I dug graves for them, and buried them there. You traitor! May your powers run dry! A curse on you, and a curse on your magic!'

'Penne! Don't try to fool me. Didn't you counter my mantra and bring them back to life?'

'Aiyo! How did you learn this?'

'I'm blessed not only with drishti but also divya drishti—my vision is complemented by divine insight. I can see things from a hundred kaadhams away with my inner eye.'

'If that's the case, why did you ask me?'

'To put you to the test. Tell me where you've hidden them Or I'll burn the two of you down to a heap of ashes!' Ravidasan said, his eyes blazing.

Poonguzhali remained silent.

'What are you waiting for? Will you tell me the truth or not? Om hreem hraam vashat ... wait, I'm going to prove my powers to you!'

Poonguzhali started trembling now. She held on tight to Senthan Amudan as if from fear, and whispered to him, 'I'm going to make a run for it. See if you can hold him back.' She then cried, 'No, please, don't do anything to me! I'll show you where they are! Come with me!'

And Poonguzhali began to walk in the direction exactly opposite to that of the ruin. The mantravadi turned to follow, and Senthan Amudan pounced on him from the back. All it took was one mighty shrug, and the mantravadi had freed himself. Poonguzhali was running now, and Ravidasan followed.

She ran like a deer, agile and fleet-footed. Ravidasan played the hunter. But it was no easy task to stop this doe. Just as he was about to give up, Poonguzhali paused as if she was tired too. He started chasing her again. Senthan Amudan ran well behind the two of them, slipping and sliding as he strove to catch up. He wondered several times whether he would not do better to run to the ruin and warn Vandiyadevan and the prince. But how could he leave Poonguzhali to the tender mercies of Ravidasan?

Poonguzhali finally reached the crest of a hill, and turned to motion the mantravadi forward.

Panting, Ravidasan climbed the hill. He was aching to slap her across both cheeks. The moment he was within earshot, she pointed and said, 'There, look, those are my lovers!'

Ravidasan stared. He saw the flames Vandiyadevan had seen, a terrifying sight compounded by the 'gub-gub' noise they made. He knew what caused this phenomenon. And yet, his hair stood on end.

'Mantravadi! If you really are as powerful as you claim to be, surely you can do something about these kolli vaai pisaasus? They're giving me hell!' Poonguzhali said.

Ravidasan was spluttering with rage. 'Penne! You think you can trick me?' he roared.

'Why would I want to trick you?'

'Didn't you bring me here promising to show me where you've hidden the prince and Vandiyadevan?'

'What option did I have, after you refused to believe my testimony that they were dead?'

'Is it really true that the prince is dead? Will you swear by it?'

'That won't be necessary. Look up at the sky.'

Ravidasan looked, as a comet shot past.

'Don't you see the shooting star? Don't you know that means a royal death has occurred?'

'Penne! In that case, let me have some of the water you're carrying with you. The run has made me thirsty.'

Poonguzhali began to run yet again. She made right for the kolli vaai pisaasus. Ravidasan was so furious that all he could think of was to catch up with her and strangle her. He jumped off the ledge as she had done and followed blindly. Poonguzhali flew through the undergrowth. Suddenly, having slowed until Ravidasan was at her heels, she skirted around something. Her pursuer was going too fast to make the same diversion. His momentum carried him right to the centre of the spot she had skirted. Ravidasan found he was no longer able to follow her. His legs would not move. What had happened, he wondered. Why were his legs numb all of a sudden? Why, the soil was rising! No, his legs were sinking! Ravidasan looked down, and realised he was trapped in quicksand. Atom by atom, inch by inch, his legs were being sucked into the earth. He would be buried alive!

Horrified, Ravidasan made a lunge for safety. But the harder he tried, the faster he sank. He had a vision of a monster hiding under the slush, holding his feet and pulling him down.

Poonguzhali was laughing.

'Mantravadi! Why are you so scared? Have you got caught in the monster's mouth? Why don't you use your magic and get out of this scrape?' she called.

Ravidasan shook as much from rage as from fear.

'Adi paavi! You planned this all along, didn't you?' he cried, knitting his fingers together in frustration.

'You wanted to strangle me, didn't you?' Poonguzhali laughed. 'There, strangle the air now, that's all you can do.'

Ravidasan did his best to hide his rage and negotiate with her. 'Penne! I promise not to harm you. Please, give me a hand and help me on to land,' he said.

Poonguzhali held her sides as she laughed. 'I'm afraid I can't help you. Why don't you call the ghosts and ghouls who are bound to obey you? The ones you control with your magic? Where are they now? Why aren't they coming to your aid?'

Ravidasan was up to his thighs in the quicksand. His face was dark, his eyes red. He threw out his arms and held on to the firm land beyond the slush. He tried to heave himself up. But his legs wouldn't move.

'Penne! You will reap the rewards of this kind act. Help me! Save me!' he wailed.

Senthan Amudan had reached the spot by now. He understood Ravidasan's predicament in an instant. His eyes softened with compassion.

'Come, let's go!' Poonguzhali said.

'Aiyo! How can we leave him like this?'

'Why, you want to watch until his entire body sinks into the quicksand?'

'No, no! I will have nightmares for the rest of my life if we leave him like this. No, let's help him ashore and then go.'

'Aththaan! He wanted to strangle me to death!'

'God will punish him for his crimes. We must save him before we go.'

'Well, if that's what you want, give me your angavastram[7].'

Amudan passed her his angavastram. Poonguzhali tied one end of it around the base of a bush near the quicksand. She threw the other end to Ravidasan.

'Mantravadi! Catch hold of this cloth, and keep yourself alive. If you pull too hard, you'll uproot the bush. So watch how much force you use. Don't try to climb to safety yourself. Wait till someone passes this way, and ask them to help you.'

'Aiyayo! You want me to stay like this all night? I can't bear the thought! No, please, it would be better to die right away. Kill me with your own hands before you go!'

Poonguzhali ignored him. She caught hold of Senthan Amudan's hand and dragged him away from the spot. She broke into a run, taking him with her. The mantravadi's cries followed them in the still night air long after they had left the spot.

Once they were out of earshot, she turned to her cousin and said, 'Thank god you turned up! At just the right time too. What brings you here, though?'

'I didn't feel like staying on in Thanjavur after they threw me into the dungeon,' Amudan said. 'The Pazhuvoor soldiers and spies kept harassing me, and so I went to Pazhaiyarai. Kundavai Devi sent me

here. She asked me to convey to Vandiyadevan that
the prince was in great danger, and that he must be
taken to the safety of the Choodamani Viharam in
Nagapattinam. I was longing to see you and hear you
sing too, and so ...'

'What a time you've picked, to hear me sing! Ilaiya
Piraatti is right. The prince is in great danger. As if
the enemy's conspiracies were not enough, he's been
laid low by a terrible fever.'

'I noticed. Vandiyadevan and I carried him to
your secret spot. It was hard going to get him there.
Poonguzhali! The Buddhist monks at the Nagapattinam
Choodamani Viharam are expert healers. They'll cure
him one way or another!'

'But how do we get him there?'

'Through the canal, how else?'

'But how do we get through the canal? You've
gone and lost my boat!'

'No, we've only upturned it to hide it. We can
get it out in no time.'

'Then we must leave right away, when it is still
dark. We must get the prince to Nagapattinam before
dawn. But ... how will we go? The four of us won't
fit in the boat.'

'We've talked it all over, Poonguzhali.
Vandiyadevan will stay back and head to Pazhaiyarai
from here. You and I will take the prince to
Nagapattinam.'

Poonguzhali's skin tingled. Another journey with the prince! All the way to Nagapattinam, drifting along the canal. She prayed that no danger would present itself en route.

The two arrived at the hidden ruin, and Senthan Amudan banged hard against the wall.

'Who goes there?' Vandiyadevan roared.

'It's me, Senthan!'

'And who is with you?'

'My uncle's daughter.'

Vandiyadevan emerged from the entrance.

'No one else?' he asked.

'No. Why do you ask?'

'Speak softly! The prince is asleep. Some time ago, I heard footsteps. I thought it must be you, and came out of hiding. But it wasn't you. I think it was the mantravadi.'

'And then ...'

'Then, I heard you sing. Great timing, I thought, you really pick your moments to sing. Thankfully, that made the mantravadi turn back. Did you both see him?'

'We did.'

'What did you do with him?'

'I didn't do anything. She's the one who's got him up to his hip in quicksand.'

'I heard her sing too ...'

'Yes, she did sing a verse.'

'The prince came out of his delirium for a brief bit when he heard her voice. He asked who was singing, and I told him it was the boatwoman. He drifted off to sleep, listening to the song.'

Poonguzhali felt her entire body soar in song.

'She didn't stop there, did she?' Senthan Amudan said. 'She screeched like an owl too.'

'I heard that too. And I wondered what was going on. Then, I thought the two of you—aththaan and his uncle's daughter, after all[8]—must be making the most of the springtime twilight.'

'What nonsense you talk!' Poonguzhali said.

'How else does one while the night away?' Vandiyadevan said.

'No, we have no time to while the night away. We cannot be here at daybreak. There is no way we will escape with our lives if we linger. We must leave by night,' Poonguzhali said.

Just then, a pack of jackals began to howl in the distance. A lone screech interrupted the siren.

Senthan Amudan shivered. In his mind's eyes, he saw the jackals closing in on the trapped mantravadi, and the man screeching like an owl in a desperate attempt to drive them away.

He busied himself helping Vandiyadevan carry the prince gently, careful not to wake him. Poonguzhali followed them.

When they reached the bank of the culvert, they laid the prince down against a tree, and asked Poonguzhali to stand guard. The two men then lowered themselves into the water. Poonguzhali watched by moonlight as they heaved the boat back up and dragged it with great effort to the shore.

The prince's eyelids fluttered open. He said hoarsely, 'I'm thirsty …'

Poonguzhali reached for the milk she had brought for him and allowed him to sip it slowly.

After some time, the prince said, 'Poonguzhali, is it really you? I thought I'd died and gone to Swargaloka, where an apsara was feeding me nectar …'

8

'AIYO! PISAASU!'

The Kalpavriksha[1] rained flowers down on Poonguzhali, even as the musical instruments of Devalokam began to play. Why, Poonguzhali's very nerves had turned into the strings of a yazh[2] and were strumming from the vibrations of the prince's lovely words.

'Ilavarase! I'm no apsara from Devalokam. I'm just a poor boat-girl. And this is no nectar. It is milk from the Kuzhagar temple.'

'You can claim you're no apsara, but how can I not believe you're a divine maiden? Are you not the daughter of Varuna himself? Aren't you Samudra Kumari? How many times you've saved my life! How will I ever pay you back?' the prince said.

'Aiya! All I want is to spend another night and another day by your side,' Poonguzhali said.

'But that is impossible! I must leave for Pazhaiyarai right away,' the prince said.

'No, we have been asked to take you to Nagapattinam.'

'By whom?'

'By Ilaiya Piraatti.'

'Who is that other man? The one who is dragging the boat here along with Vandiyadevan?'

'My aththaan, Senthan Amudan. He is the one through whom Ilaiya Piraatti sent word. She wants us to take you to the Choodamani Viharam in Nagapattinam.'

'Aha! So my sister has changed her mind, then? She no longer wants to crown me king? For the longest time, I have yearned to join the Buddhist order. I would like to become a monk. I will journey to faraway lands. To Savagam and Kadaram and Maayirudingam and Maabappaalam and Cheenam. Aha! What a fortunate man I am! Come, Poonguzhali, let us go!' the prince said, and stood up.

Poonguzhali suspected he wasn't quite himself, that it was the delirium that dictated his thoughts and actions.

At that very moment, a cry rent the air from far away.

The prince stood startled, and then asked, 'Poonguzhali! What is that?'

'Just the screech of an owl, aiya!' she said.

'No! It is a human voice! Someone who is in great danger, screaming for help. We must go and save him right away. That would be an auspicious start to my journey into monkhood. One good deed before I even enter the order!' the prince said joyously, and made as if to run, only to trip and fall. Poonguzhali lunged forward to hold him before he hit the ground.

Vandiyadevan and Senthan Amudan, having just anchored the boat, came running to help. The prince had lost consciousness again. They lifted him on to their shoulders carefully, and lowered him on to the boat as gently as they could. Then, they began to sail down the culvert. The boat was not made for four people. The prince occupied most of the space, and the other three felt suffocated.

'Poonguzhali,' Vandiyadevan said. 'This boat cannot carry four people. I must take your leave anyway and I might as well do it now. I'll get off here and make my way. I leave it to the two of you to take the prince to the viharam. I need hardly give you instructions. You know all I do and more.'

His voice was shaking. When the rays of the moon cut through the canopy, Poonguzhali saw the tears shine bright in his eyes.

'Why don't you get off once we cross the Kodikkarai forest? I've left my horse there. You remember the spot, don't you?' Senthan Amudan said.

'No, I think it's better I take your leave right here. I will rest for a while in the Kuzhagar temple, and then leave before dawn. Otherwise, I'll be too tired for the journey. Who knows what obstacles await?'

Poonguzhali suddenly remembered the prasadam she had miraculously managed to hang on to all through the adventures of the night.

'Here, this is the prasadam from the temple. Eat this before you sleep,' she said.

'But neither of you has eaten. Won't you have some?'

'There are a whole lot of villages on the way. We'll get food there. One of us can go door to door and ask. But you can't be seen by anyone before you reach Pazhaiyarai.'

'Yes, but don't forget the prince is on the boat with you. You're in no less danger than I am.'

'Who will believe this is the prince? Don't worry about that. He is our responsibility now. And no one will pay this dilapidated boat any attention.'

'Well, then, I'll get off here.'

Just then, they heard the pained cry yet again.

'Aha! What is that? Who is that?' the prince asked, opening his eyes.

Poonguzhali stood up.

'I can't do this anymore. The prince will never forgive me if he finds out what I've done. I'll have to pull that mantravadi out before we go. Stay for a while longer on the boat. I'll be right back. The spot isn't far from here,' Poonguzhali said, and leapt nimbly onto the shore.

'I'll go with you,' Senthan Amudan said. 'I can't leave you alone with that dangerous man.'

'No, Amuda! You stay on the boat and guard the prince. I'll go with Poonguzhali. I have some business with the mantravadi myself!' Vandiyadevan said, and jumped off the boat. He ran behind Poonguzhali as she wove through the trees.

Poonguzhali was haunted by a vision of the mantravadi, sunk chest deep in quicksand as jackals closed in on him. What a terrible death! The prince would look at her accusingly and say, 'You are a murderess!' No, no, she could not let that happen! The fear sent a burst of energy through her body, and her legs went faster than ever.

She reached the spot in no time, and then stared in surprise. The mantravadi was missing.

When Vandiyadevan caught up with her, he saw why she had stopped short.

'It must be another patch of quicksand. They're all over the place, no? You must have got confused,' he said.

Silent, Poonguzhali could only point at the angavastram she had tied to the bush. The poor girl had lost her powers of speech.

'You think he sank in the quicksand? No, no! Ravidasan can't be killed that easily! He has a hundred lives. He would have escaped,' Vandiyadevan said, as he untied the angavastram.

He didn't believe his own words, though. He was trying to comfort Poonguzhali, but in his heart of hearts, he knew there was little chance of Ravidasan having escaped. Well, he deserved this death.

There was little point in lingering there. So, Vandiyadevan and Poonguzhali made for the canal again.

The trees grew thick by the bank. As they approached, they saw two figures peering into the culvert, holding on to the branches of the trees. One was a man, and the other appeared to be a woman.

'There, look!' Poonguzhali said, pointing.

'Yes, I see. Can you tell who they are?'

'One is the mantravadi. The woman is my brother's wife. She's come here and freed the mantravadi before I got to the spot!'

'Well, that's all good, then.'

'There is no good in it! They've spotted the boat, don't you see?'

Even as Poonguzhali spoke, both figures turned as one and looked in her direction. They then disappeared into the brush.

'Aiyo! They've spotted us as well now!'

'Keep quiet and follow my lead. I've got a plan. Whatever I say, don't react with surprise. Just go with it,' Vandiyadevan said.

They reached the spot where they had spied the two figures. Vandiyadevan went a little ahead and sat by the bank. He made sure his voice would carry to the two people hiding in the bushes, and began to speak.

'Listen, Poonguzhali, there's no need to worry,' he said. 'So, the mantravadi is dead! Good! It's better that way, isn't it?'

'Aiyo! But what a horrible death!' Poonguzhali said, catching on.

'What's the point of pity after committing murder?'

'Aiyo! You're calling me a murderer?'

'Who conned him into falling in the quicksand? It was you, wasn't it? You felt the prick of conscience after and came to save his life. But the quicksand beat you to him, and swallowed him up before you could act on your instincts. Well, assuming you really wanted to save him. For all I know, you simply came to make sure he'd died.'

'Why did you follow me here?'

'It was because I followed you that I found out just what you had done. What brutality!'

'I'm a brute, now?'

'Yes, indeed you are! A brute! A brutal murderess!'

'*I*? A brutal murderess!'

'Of course! I don't claim to be a saint, do I? I drowned the prince at sea, and you sank the mantravadi in mud. We're quite even then. If you won't tell anyone about the murder I committed, I won't tell anyone about the murder you committed.'

'It was *you* who killed the prince? But you said just now that you haven't seen him?'

'I lied. But I don't have to worry about you anymore. We have a deal, don't we?'

'What if I say we don't?'

'I'll go and tell Nandini Devi right away what you've done. There is no evidence of the murder I've committed. But there is proof of what you have done.'

'What will Nandini do to me, anyway?'

'Oh, nothing much. She'll just have you buried up to the neck, and then have an elephant trample your head.'

'What! What a terrible death!'

'If you want to evade that fate, you must do as I say.'

'What must I do?'

'There, you see your aththaan bringing a boat? Get on it and head for Lanka. Go there and cry for your prince!'

'Why must I go to Lanka? What does it matter to you if I stay here?'

'How do I know you won't go and tell Periya Pazhuvettaraiyar about what I've done? He does love the prince very much, whatever his stance might be about the rightful heir. He will seek to avenge his death. I can't die so soon, I have things to do!'

'Ada paavi! But why did you kill the prince? At least tell me that! I don't understand a thing!'

'What do I have to lose? I might as well tell you. The prince and his sister were plotting to steal Aditya Karikalar's title from him. Aditya Karikalar is my leader and commander. He is the master, and I am his servant. His enemies are my enemies. Do you see now why I had to kill the prince?'

'You've committed a terrible sin. You will pay the price for it!'

'Don't worry your head about that. Now, tell me once and for all—will you do as I say or not?'

'Do I have a choice? Well, the boat is nearly here. I'll get on it.'

'Listen carefully, now! The moment you get on the boat, you must make for the ocean. You dare turn back to Kodikkarai, you'll be done for! I'll stay here and keep watch until your boat reaches the sea, you hear? I won't leave before I make sure you've done as I said!'

'Fine, fine, have it your way! Stay here! I hope a thousand jackals tear you to pieces!' Poonguzhali said, and got to her feet at a discreet signal from Vandiyadevan. She hurried towards the boat.

Vandiyadevan kept watch as he had said he would, as Poonguzhali got on it and began to row. The boat went far down the canal, and eventually disappeared from sight. Half a naazhigai had passed since they had parted.

All of a sudden, a loud guffaw made its way from the brush.

Vandiyadevan scrambled to his feet as if startled and looked around in a great show of panic.

The mantravadi emerged from the bushes. Looking at Vandiyadevan, he laughed like a banshee.

'Aiyo! Pisaasu!'[3] Vandiyadevan screamed, and took to his heels.

9

THREE PEOPLE IN A BOAT

As the dawn broke, the dusky goddess of night had to leave her lover, the earth. Her heart was not in it. The fingers that had been caressing her lover lingered on even as they tried to wrench themselves away from his skin. She kissed him as if it was the last kiss of her life, loathe to let go.

'We're going to meet in the evening, after all. Our separation is only for four jaamams[1], isn't it? Why are you so forlorn? Smile for me now, and come back when you can!' the earth said.

The night moved away, but she walked away reluctantly, turning back every now and again to catch a glimpse of the earth she loved so dearly.

The moment her back was turned, though, the earth turned a cad who was incapable of feeling true love and forced to make a pretence of it so he could have his way with women. He jumped for joy at his newfound freedom. He sent thousands of birds flying into air, singing for joy. Buds blossomed into flowers on trees and shrubs. Bees arrived in hordes to burrow into the parted petals of flowers, humming and buzzing. Butterflies with their myriad colours painted the world with beauty.

As the golden sun rose, the stars disappeared one by one. The moon god paused in his tracks and wondered whether he should stay or leave.

The boat was floating gently. Poonguzhali heard the soft splash of water against the oars, which interrupted the song of the birds. She opened her eyes, realising she had fallen asleep only when she woke.

O reader, let me take a moment to describe the loveliness of those eyes—they were as two dark blue blossoms unfurling their petals at once, side by side on a tree branch.

And even as we admire her eyes, she took in one sight alone—the prince's beloved face. He was still asleep. Was it sleep or unconsciousness, she wondered. She couldn't tell. But how radiant he was! How his face glowed in the morning light!

Senthan Amudan was plying the oars.

'Poonguzhali, why don't you sleep a while longer?' he asked.

Poonguzhali smiled. It wasn't just her mouth but her entire body that smiled. She was a creature of the forest. She had grown up among its trees and birds. And yet, their song had never sounded as melodious as it did that day.

'Aththaan! Why don't you sing a song in the morning raga?' she asked.

'Sing when you're here? I wouldn't dare!' Amudan said. 'You sing.'

'You sang in the forest last night, no? Why don't you sing?'

'I was compelled by the circumstances last night. You sing now.'

'I do feel like singing. But what if I disturb the prince?'

'It will not disturb me. Go on, both of you sing,' Arulmozhi Varmar said.

Poonguzhali blushed at the thought that he had been watching and listening all along.

'Where is the boat headed?' the prince asked.

'To the Choodamani Viharam in Nagapattinam,' Poonguzhali said.

'Oh, so it wasn't all a dream? I didn't imagine it? What I saw and heard at night ... that was real?'

'Yes, aiya, indeed it was! This is Amudan. He's the one who brought a message from your sister.'

'Amuda, tell me in detail what Ilaiya Piraatti said. Did she command me to join the Buddhist order?'

Senthan Amudan was wondering how to respond, when they heard the sound of hooves. Poonguzhali and Senthan Amudan were startled. The prince's expression remained unchanged.

'Where is my friend? The hero of the Vaanar clan?' he asked.

Before they could answer, the prince closed his eyes again.

As if he had been conjured into existence, Vandiyadevan arrived on horseback. What a relief, Poonguzhali thought, that he was the horseman who had scared them moments earlier.

'I just came to check on you before I carry on,' he said.

'What became of the mantravadi?' Poonguzhali asked.

'He doesn't have the slightest suspicion that the prince might be on the boat. He believed my words fully.'

'Did you see him?'

'Yes, but I made a show of thinking he was a pisaasu and ran away as if in fright.'

'I've never met so skilled a liar as you!'

'Don't call it lies. Call it imagination. How is the prince doing?'

'He wakes up every now and again, speaks a sentence or two and then drifts back into sleep.'

'That is the nature of this illness.'

'How long will it last?'

'It can drag on for up to a month. But don't worry. All you need to do is hand him over to the monks at the Choodamani Viharam. They will ensure he is cured in a couple of weeks. Be wary, Poonguzhali. I'm trusting the prince's safety to you. Your aththaan is scatterbrained. If he so much as chances upon a temple gopuram, he'll wander off for a darshan of the deity, singing his way to the temple.'

'I won't do any such thing now. Meeting you has robbed me of those notions. Even my desire to serve Shiva is gone now,' Senthan Amudan said.

'Is it really I who have lured you away from your austere life? Is it not this woman? Tell us the truth now!'

Senthan Amudan said as if Vandiyadevan had not spoken at all, 'Did you find the horse where I said you would?'

'The horse found me. This is the same horse I left with you in Thanjai, no?'

'Yes.'

'He spotted me in the darkness of the night, in the thick of the forest, and whinnied for me. Amuda, you know, I learnt something when I was imprisoned by the Arabs. I believe it is cruel to make horses ride barefoot. They have iron shields to protect their hooves. I'm going to get this done at the first ironsmith's workshop I see. Well, anyway, there's no time for idle conversation of this sort. I don't know whether I'll meet you both or the prince anytime soon. If he wakes again, tell him I've gone to Pazhaiyarai, and will send word to him as soon as I can. He won't know peace unless you tell him this.'

Vandiyadevan took his leave and rode off on his horse. It wasn't long before he disappeared.

Thazhampoo shrubs lined the canal. There were two varieties, one with golden yellow blossoms and another with ivory white flowers. Their fragrance was intoxicating. These shrubs were interspersed with kadamba trees that scattered their kumkum-coloured flowers on the forest floor, and punnai trees adorned with pearl-like flowers. The path from earth to Heaven must be like this, Poonguzhali thought.

Every time they saw a village in the distance, Amudan would anchor the boat and go there. He would return with food for Poonguzhali and milk for the prince.

Whenever Arulmozhi Varmar woke, Poonguzhali moved as far away as she could and avoided making eye contact with him. When he fell asleep, she drank in his face and its features. She and Senthan Amudan spoke about various things, and sang together every now and again.

In the intervals when Amudan disappeared into the villages and she was alone with the prince, Poonguzhali laid his head on her lap and stroked his forehead and caressed his hair. Her heart was full, her body alive. She knew true elation. It was as if time had stopped. She could see every previous birth of hers, births she had spent in the company of the prince, serving him. A million memories from lifetimes of long ago flew into her head and beat their wings so hard that her heart raced.

They spent a day and a night rowing through the canal. Poonguzhali and Senthan Amudan took turns plying the oars, each cousin allowing the other to sleep. Poonguzhali dreamt the sweetest dreams of her life through that day.

At daybreak, when the entire world had turned golden from the sun's softest rays, they came across a fork in the waterway. One branch led straight to the Choodamani Viharam. They rowed down that culvert and anchored the boat by the backyard of the viharam.

There seemed to be a grand commotion there. A throng of people was assembled, and they seemed to be agitated, shouting and screaming. The monks ran about in seeming consternation.

All three occupants of the boat disembarked. Senthan Amudan said he would head to the viharam and figure out what was happening.

10

THE CHOODAMANI VIHARAM

The ancient town of Kaveripattinam, as Poompuhar was then called, had been destroyed by the sea, as readers are aware.[1] The mantle of the most important port in Chozha Naadu was then handed over to Nagapattinam. People sailed from faraway kingdoms to establish trade relations with the lush land of Chozha Naadu, its natural beauty tended by the Ponni river. Enormous ships carrying pearls and rubies and diamonds and perfumes stood alongside Arab vessels bearing horses for sale.

Nagapattinam had gained great prestige in Sundaramurti's time. Nambi Aroorar[2], wrote, on his visit:

Kaanbiniya manimaadam niraindha nedu veedhi
Kadal nagai karonam mevi irundheere

In the wide avenues lined with grand mansions
Of the port city, you lived, gracing Nagai Karonam

So he sang, of the Karona Perumal—or the Kayarohana Perumal—who lived in the temple of Nagapattinam.[3] And do you know what he asked of this god? Not just the usual gold and gems and clothes and vestments but also a thoroughbred Arab horse, all duly granted![4]

The Periyapuranam recounts this incident as:

Nambithaamum annaatpoyi Nagai Karonam paadi
Amponmanipoonnavamanigal aadai saantham
adarparima

And Nambi went to that land and sang the praises of
Nagai Karonam
And got for reward, along with gold and gems
And clothes and the navaratna, an Arab stallion

Clearly, even Shaivite saints are not exempt from being tempted to ride a horse when their eyes fall on an Arab thoroughbred! Nagapattinam is not extolled simply in literature; we have historical evidence, in the form of etchings on copper plates and edicts on the walls of temples, that describe the ancient city in all its glory. The ones recovered from Anaimangalam, for instance, tell us that the town had many temples and squares and ponds and lakes and irrigation canals that fed fields and gardens some distance from the wide main streets, which were lined with the aforementioned mansions. These copper plates also detail the Choodamani Viharam's grand stature at the time, as well as its history.

The region we know today as the Malay Peninsula was known as Srivijaya Naadu back in the day. Kadaram[5] was an important town in that land. The Srivijaya empire was held by the Shailendra dynasty, which had made Kadaram its capital. One of the most famous kings of this dynasty was Makaradhwaja[6] Choodamani Varman. The copper plates of Anaimangalam speak of him as an astute ruler: 'As wise and learned as Brihaspati, he was to scholars as the sun is to lotuses, a Kalpavriksha to the mendicant.'[7]

The son of this great ruler was Maravijayottunga Varman, and the etchings on copper plates say he sought to preserve his father's legacy by building the Choodamani Viharam 'as tall as the Meru peak'.

Of course, readers might wonder why the ruler of Kadaram came all the way to Nagapattinam to build a viharam in his father's honour. You see, Srivijaya Naadu was among the kingdoms to have the strongest ties with Chozha Naadu. The people of that land often travelled to Chozha Naadu, and many even settled in Nagapattinam. The king and his people were Buddhists, and so Vijayottunga Varman built the viharam so that his subjects would have a place of worship in their adopted land. Perhaps the fact that India was the birthplace of Buddhism had also been on the king's mind. The kings of Tamizhagam had always been tolerant and even welcoming of other religions, and so they readily gave him permission to build the Choodamani Viharam in Nagapattinam. And they didn't stop there. They often made donations of gold and irayili land[8] to the viharam. (Long after our story ends, Raja Raja Chozhan would grant the entire village of Anaimangalam and its surrounding regions as irayili to the viharam. This donation has been documented by his son, Rajendra Chozhan, on copper plates. It was these famous copper plates that were discovered at Anaimangalam. There were twenty-one of them, fourteen inches long and five inches wide, bound by a copper ring bearing the Chozha royal insignia. These plates have crossed the seas and are preserved at the city of Leiden in Holland. One can see them at the university of that city. Some historians now refer to the Anaimangalam copper plates as the 'Leiden Plates'.)

Ever since the reign of Vijayalaya Chozhar, the Chozha kings had been great devotees of Shiva. Aditya Chozhar, Parantaka Chozhar and Kandaradityar set aside large sums for service to the deities of the various Shiva temples, and for the expansion and ornamentation of those temples. Yet, they were not prejudiced against other religions. They ruled impartially, treating their subjects as equal irrespective of religious persuasion.

Sundara Chozhar was a few steps ahead of his predecessors. He made generous donations to Buddhist institutions. This warmed the hearts of the Buddhists in his land and outside. Arulmozhi Varmar's orders to renovate or rebuild the destroyed viharams in Lanka would go on to seal their loyalties to the Chozha clan.

In this context, why was there such a commotion at the Choodamani Viharam? Why were the monks running helter-skelter, instead of going about their work calmly? What did the crowd gathered at its entrance want? Why all the yelling and screaming? Well, there's only one way to find out. Let's follow Senthan Amudan and see.

Readers will remember that the trio in the boat had arrived practically at the backyard of the Choodamani Viharam. Senthan Amudan got off the boat, but couldn't find anyone who would guide him. He stumbled and fumbled and eventually found his way to the entrance.

This was the spot where devotees gathered of a morning to pray to the Buddha statue. They brought lotuses and shenbagham flowers and other offerings. That day was no different, except it appeared the devotees had forgotten why they had arrived at the temple. The monks were gathered at the steps leading up to the viharam. Someone in the crowd was addressing them. Senthan Amudan observed that some of the monks' eyes were glistening with tears. And in place of the usual 'Saathu, Saathu', cries of 'Aahaa!', 'Adadaa!' and 'Aiyo!' rose into the air.

Once he got closer, he understood what the matter was. The man speaking to the monks was one of Parthibendran's sailors. The rumours of the prince's drowning had arrived with the ship the previous night. It was to ascertain the truth of this that the head priest of the viharam had sent for one of the sailors. He confirmed their worst fears, saying in a shaking voice, 'The prince jumped into the sea in the middle of the storm, and never returned.'

At these words, wails rose afresh from the crowd. Tears began to pour from the eyes of the head priest. He turned back without a word, his head bowed in sorrow. The other monks turned as one and followed him into the viharam. No one noticed that Senthan Amudan had taken his place among them.

The head priest addressed them.

'Is this all the compassion Lord Buddha has shown?' he said. 'I'd built castles in the air. I'd gone to Thanjavur to meet the emperor. I told him of Arulmozhi Varmar's incredible deeds in Lanka. Ilaiya Piraatti Kundavai Devi was listening too. Then, she called me aside and told me she wanted to start an aadurasalai in the viharam and was happy to provide all that was required for this. And that was not all.

'She said, "Aasiriyare[9]! You must have heard of all the rumours afloat. If it so happens that the prince should visit the Choodamani Viharam as a guest for a while, would you be able to shelter and protect him?"

'"Devi!" I said. "If we were to be blessed with such an honour, we would protect him as the eyelid protects the eye!"

'What is the point of it all? Was it simply the prince who has drowned? The dreams and desires of all good men have drowned! The very Chozha empire has drowned! How could Samudra Raja bring himself to commit such a heinous crime! Is there no one who will question him?'

The other monks stood silent, tears streaming down their faces.

Senthan Amudan decided this was the right moment to speak, and wound his way to the front.

Several of the monks stepped before him to stop his progress, even as they turned to each other in puzzlement.

'Who is this?'

'How did he get here?'

'Who let him in?'

'Aiya, my name is Senthan Amudan. I have something to tell the head priest.'

'Tell us, tell us!' many of the monks chorused.

The head priest noticed his hesitation and said, 'What you can tell me, you can tell them. Please go ahead.'

'Aiya! I have brought an ailing man.'

'Who is this ailing man? And what is the illness? Where have you left him?'

'At the backyard of the viharam.'

'How did you get there?'

'Through the canal. I brought him here by boat. He is shivering with fever. If you would come right away and ...'

'Bhagavaane! That fever is contagious! Why did you bring him here? And what a time to pick!'

'Aasiriyare! I thought thus far that Emperor Ashoka was a Buddhist. I see now that I was mistaken.'

'Why do you say that?'

'I saw an Ashoka stupa near Kanchi. The inscription says the first duty of a follower of this religion is to cure the sick. But here you are, chasing me away!' Amudan said.

At this, the head priest addressed his assembly and said, 'Give me a moment. Let me go see what the matter is.' He then turned to Amudan and said, 'Appane! Lead the way.'

As they approached the spot, the head priest saw that a young man and woman were there and was horrified. 'What have you done!' he shouted at Senthan. 'Women are not allowed on these premises! Why, even the bhikkunis[10] have a separate mutth all to themselves!'

But a bigger shock awaited him when he went closer and recognised the youth. To say the monk was rendered speechless would not quite capture the moment. It would be more accurate to say he was stupefied from surprise and delight.

He turned to Senthan Amudan and gasped, 'Is it really Prince Arulmozhi Varmar?'

His words fell on the prince's ears. 'No,' he said, 'not at all, asiriyare. I'm not a prince, I'm not anything at all. This girl and this boy are conspiring to drive me insane. I'm a boatman. Just a while ago, I asked this woman, "Penne! Will you marry me? Let us sail to faraway lands together." And she went on blabbering about something. She claims I was born to bring the world under the same umbrella. She says she's a poor girl from a fisherman's family, and will not marry me. All that matters to her is my comfort and happiness. And she will hear tell of my great exploits and derive joy from that. What nonsense! Who is hallucinating, I or she?'

Senthan Amudan whispered something to the head priest. But the priest had already discerned that the prince was delirious. He remembered Kundavai Devi's request.

The head priest returned to the assembly and told the monks, 'The boy does have the fever and chills that have been killing our men in Lanka. If we cast him out, he will infect thousands of others. So, we will keep him here and cure him. I will take him to my room and tend to him myself. Remember that he is delirious. So, if you should hear him mumble something, please don't take it seriously.'

He went back to the prince and gently lifted him. Senthan Amudan helped the priest, and together they climbed the stairs leading into the viharam.

Poonguzhali stood watching. There, in a few moments they would have climbed to the top of the stairs. Then, they would open the door and enter the viharam. The door would close. And she would never see the prince again.

She watched as they reached the top of the stairs. The head priest turned to Senthan Amudan and said something. Then, they entered the viharam and the door closed behind them.

It was as if a door had banged shut right on her heart. Something inside her shrivelled.

There was little chance she would see the prince again in this lifetime, she thought. Would she have the fortune to meet him in another birth, at least?

11

AT THE IRONMONGER'S

Vandiyadevan rode towards Pazhaiyarai. He remembered the way to an extent, and chose to go by instinct rather than stop and ask passers-by for directions. For a while, he kept to the forest paths, but sensed that the rough terrain was terribly hard on his horse's bare hooves. He was sleepy himself. He couldn't remember the last time he had had a good night's rest. He had only snatched the odd hour of sleep when his eyelids would drop shut of their own accord and he could no longer move. Once he had reached Pazhaiyarai and given the princess the news, he would have time to sleep. He would make up for all these days of sleeplessness, he thought. He would give himself a week, perhaps a fortnight, of continuous deep sleep.

He would tell Kundavai Devi, 'I have fulfilled the promises I made you. I have accomplished the mission on which you sent me.'

What joy it would give him! Her face would glow as she heard the words. The idea gave him gooseflesh.

A not-so-happy memory surfaced too. He thought to himself of the many lies he had told since he had left Kanchipuram. He had twisted the truth on the odd occasion he hadn't resorted to outright lies. Well, it was true he had only turned to deception when the need had arisen, but would his friend Arulmozhi Varmar have approved, he wondered.

The time he had spent in the prince's company had changed his outlook. Earlier, he had believed that those who handled governance ought to have Chanakya's cunning. And this cunning, he had thought, would win him back the kingdom his ancestors had lost. But all that had changed now. The prince's straightforwardness and honesty had given him a disgust of deception.

He then thought of the lie he had spoken just the previous day, to fool the mantravadi and save the prince. He hoped nothing disastrous would come of his words. What if someone else had overheard him? What if someone had gone and told Kundavai Devi of it? No, Ilaiya Piraatti would never believe it! Even so, what a risk he had taken!

He would never again do such a thing. No more fictions. He would only speak the truth. And whatever came of it, he would face the consequences. He would leave it to the likes of the Veera Vaishnavan Azhvarkadiyaan and Ravidasan to play the spy. It was not a role that suited him. He was made for the sword and spear, for open battle, not hidden agendas. He was done with it all.

Preoccupied as he was with these thoughts, it took him a while to notice that his horse had slowed down. His eyelids had begun to droop too. It was only when the horse stumbled that he woke with a start.

He realised his horse was struggling to walk on one of his forelegs. Vandiyadevan slid off the horse, patted the animal and checked the leg. A sharp stone had lodged itself in the hoof. He carefully removed the stone. What a relief, it was only a minor injury. As he comforted his horse with a rub and then got back on his ride, he thought back to the Arab sailors' words:

'The people of Tamizhagam are savages. And have no brains either! They make their horses run barefoot, without shoes. How long will such horses live?'

This thought haunted him as he rode. Soldiers never entered the battlefield without armour. Yes, the thought of armour for the horses' feet was rather bizarre. But he had heard of this even before he had encountered the Arabs. He had heard tell of lands where horses were given shoes to protect their hooves. He decided he would stop at the first ironmonger's workshop he saw, and make enquiries about shoeing the horse. If he wasn't able to do this, there wasn't much chance the horse would make it to Pazhaiyarai. What if the animal collapsed en route? He would have to earn money to buy another horse. And how would he do that under his circumstances? His only choice then would be to steal one. Chhi, chhi! What an ugly thought! He felt ashamed of himself for even considering it.

He led the horse out of the forest and on to the rajpath. He would stick to this wide road and face whatever came his way. There wasn't much chance he would be recognised on this route. The entourage of the Pazhuvettaraiyar brothers would not pass this way for some time. Neither would the mantravadi. So, there was little danger. Besides, how would he find an ironmonger's workshop in the forest?

His hopes were not in vain. It wasn't long before he arrived at a village.

He sensed a buzz in the air. Many of the houses had been ornamented with strings of flowers and thoranams. Perhaps they were expecting the Pazhuvettaraiyar entourage here. Well, he would be long gone before they came.

There were groups of men and women and children about, and the conversation appeared to be hurried and anxious. Vandiyadevan was not able to figure out what the matter was. When they saw him, some people broke off and hurried towards the horse, as if to stop him and ask him something. Vandiyadevan ignored them and rode faster. He didn't want to be drawn into anything right then.

Once he had passed the village, he saw an ironmonger's workshop by the side of the road. He dismounted the horse and went inside.

The ironmonger was at work. Vandiyadevan noticed a little boy inside, fiddling with some sort of instrument. Even as he entered, it struck him that someone was hurrying out from the backdoor. But these were things that his brain observed, without his mind processing it, because all his attention was on one sole object.

The sword in the ironmonger's hands mesmerised him.

It was an incredible sword. It appeared the ironmonger was sharpening it. Part of the sword shone like silver. The other part, fresh from the furnace, glowed red.

Now, *this* was a sword!

12

'THROW THEM IN THE FIRE!'

The ironmonger was so preoccupied with his work that Vandiyadevan had to clear his throat several times to catch his attention. The man finally looked up.

'Who are you, appane? What would you like? A sword? A spear? Well, what use does one have for either these days? It's not likely you want me to forge a sword for you,' the ironmonger said.

'What are you saying, aiya? You have a sword in hand, and yet you ask what use one has for swords!' Vandiyadevan said.

'Oh, this was a one-off. They brought me this sword and wanted me to polish and sharpen it,' the ironmonger said. 'Some years ago, when the war against Pandiya Naadu and the Vada Pennai war were on, there were mountains of swords and spears here. Even at the start of the war in Lanka, weapons were brought here to be sharpened. But, these days, no one seems to want arms. They, in fact, bring me old swords and spears to sell. Perhaps that is what brings you here?'

'No, no, I will have use for my sword for a good few years. Once I'm done with the battlefield, I plan to get a pair of cymbals and walk the streets, singing the devaaram and visiting temples. Before I take off on this pilgrimage, I'll bring all my weapons to you.'

'What brings you here today, then?'

'I've ridden my horse through forests and fields, hills and valleys. And we have a long distance to go yet. Apparently, one can make a horseshoe from iron. Do you think you can do this?'

'Yes, apparently, that is the norm in Arabia. Some people have taken to it here as well. I've done it before.'

'Will you make a shoe for my horse, then?'

'That will take a while. I cannot start on your commission until I've finished the work at hand.'

Vandiyadevan thought about it. He was exhausted. The horse was drained. He might as well wait for a while, and rest until the shoes had been fitted.

'All right, I'll wait until you're done. But will you do my work right after?'

'Of course!'

Vandiyadevan sat down to wait, but he couldn't tear his eyes away from the sword.

'The work on this sword is exquisite. Whose is it?' he asked.

'Appane! Some distance from here is the Arichandra[1] River.'

'So I've heard. What of it?'

'It is my wont to take a dip in it every now and again.'

'Excellent. You carry those good vibes everywhere you go, then.'

'And so, I try to tell the truth and avoid lies to the extent possible.'

'And so what? Who asked you to lie? Not I!'

'If you don't ask me any questions about this sword, I can avoid lying.'

Oho! So that's how it is, Vandiyadevan thought to himself.

'All right, I won't ask any questions, and you don't have to go against your principles. All I ask is that you finish what you're doing as soon as you can, and get started on the work I have for you.'

The ironmonger worked in silence, as Vandiyadevan sat back.

The Vaanar scion spent a while longer staring at the sword. On its pommel, just below the grip, was an etching of a fish. He was surprised by it. Was it simply ornamental or did the fish carry significance, he wondered.

The ironmonger then lowered the pommel into the furnace, hammered at it and then held it to the flame again. Clearly, he intended to erase the fish. Why was he doing such a thing? Even as Vandiyadevan was analysing this, his eyelids fluttered. Nidra Devi[2], whom he had been chasing away for days, now cast her net at him. Vandiyadevan could not evade it this time. For a while, he sat, nodding off. Then, he lay down right there, on the floor of the workshop and fell asleep. But it was not a restful sleep; he had horrifying dreams.

In one, a man came to the workshop and asked for the sword. The ironmonger handed it over. The man asked how much he owed, and the ironmonger replied, 'I don't want any fee. Let this by my offering to the Pazhuvoor Ilaiya Rani.'

'Careful! Don't breathe a word about this to anyone! Most importantly, don't ever speak the name of the Pazhuvoor Ilaiya Rani! If you do, do you know what we will do to you?'

'Why would I mention the Pazhuvoor Ilaiya Rani, aiya? I won't breathe a word to anyone.'

'There's some youth lying right here. And you've spoken her name out loud!'

'He is practically unconscious. Thunder and lightning won't wake him.'

'If you have the slightest suspicion that he has come to know of something, throw him in the furnace and be done with it!'

Then, Vandiyadevan felt himself being dragged towards the furnace by the ironmonger and the man. Before they could throw him in, though, the dream changed.

Now, Yama's men were escorting Vandiyadevan to hell.

Yama Dharmaraja enquired about his deeds on earth.

Chitragupta consulted his scroll and said, 'He is an expert liar. There is no limit to the lies he can tell. I've lost count of them.'

'No, no! Every single one of those lies was in the service of the emperor and his family. It was all to accomplish a mission for the good of everyone.'

'The intention does not matter. A lie is a lie. Go, throw him into the fires of hell!' Yama ordered.

At this, a hundred thousand voices from the interiors of hell set up a great howl.

Yama's henchmen led Vandiyadevan to the edge of a seemingly bottomless pit from which fires bigger than any he had ever imagined, let alone seen, blazed tall. As the two men readied to throw him inside, Vandiyadevan realised they were the Pazhuvettaraiyar brothers. Just as he was coming to terms with this shock, who should appear at the spot but Kundavai Devi!

'He lied only in order to follow my commands,' she said. 'Throw me in the fire in his stead.'

At this point, Nandini Devi, too, ended up there.

'Throw them both in the fire,' that good woman said.

As Yama's men held them both, Vandiyadevan screamed, 'No!' and awoke with a start.

He realised he had been dreaming. That was a comforting thought. But it had felt so real that he was still shaking.

Tchah tchah, he would never lie again, whatever the stakes were, he decided.

He then turned to the ironmonger and asked, 'Did I sleep for long?'

'Oh, no, not at all. Just a couple of jaamams[3]. Appane! Are you a descendant of Kumbhakarna? If this is how you sleep during the day, I wonder how you must sleep at night!' the ironmonger said.

'God! Was I really asleep that long? Have you finished shoeing the horse?'

'I'm yet to do that. But what's the point of shoeing the horse of a sleepyhead like you? You're simply going to lose the horse. Why, you might even lose yourself!'

Vandiyadevan jumped out of his skin. A thought suddenly occurred to him, and he ran out of the workshop. His horse was missing.

'Aiyo! Where is my horse?' he cried, reaching for his sword.

'Don't worry. Your horse is safe. Go to the backyard and see for yourself.'

Vandiyadevan ran there, and saw his horse standing in a stall improvised from three planks of wood. The little boy he had seen in the workshop when he had first arrived was feeding the horse grass. When the animal's eyes fell on his master, he neighed and shook himself as if readying himself for a journey.

'Aiya! Please come here and hold your horse. I need to take measurements for the shoe,' the boy said.

Vandiyadevan stroked the horse as the boy went about his business.

'Who brought the horse here?' Vandiyadevan asked.

'I did.'

'Why?'

'My father asked me to.'

'And why was that?'

'Periya Pazhuvettaraiyar passed through the village with his entourage. If they had seen the horse outside, they would have confiscated him.'

Vandiyadevan thought of the incident at Tirunarayanapuram, when his horse had had the misfortune of being spotted by Pazhuvettaraiyar's soldiers. What a terrible mistake he had made in leaving the animal in plain sight! He was indebted to the ironmonger and his son. Once the boy was done taking measurements, the two of them went back into the workshop.

The ironmonger took an iron rod and began to bend it to fashion the horseshoe.

'You saved my horse from being kidnapped! Thank you, more than I can say,' Vandiyadevan said.

'It is only my duty. I'm obliged to look after the belongings of those who seek me.'

'How long has it been since Pazhuvettaraiyar's entourage passed this way?' Vandiyadevan asked.

'More than two naazhigais, I should think. You slept through all the pomp and circumstance. I can barely believe it.'

'Right, so I slept off. But you wasted all that time! Why didn't you start the work I gave you, at least after they had left, if not before?'

'How could I? Who would feel like working after the news they brought? I'm forcing myself to do this work because I've already given you my word. Where have you come from, appane?'

The ironmonger was looking intently at Vandiyadevan. Then, he lowered his voice and asked, 'Did you meet the prince when you were in Lanka?'

Vandiyadevan, who had just made a resolution to only ever speak the truth, said, 'Yes, I did.'

'When did you last see him?'

'This morning.'

The ironmonger glared at him. 'Do you think this is a joke, thambi?'

'No, aiya, it is the truth.'

'It appears you will be able to tell where the prince is right now too.'

'Oh, yes, I will if you ask.'

'Fine, tell me then!'

'In the Choodamani Viharam at Nagapattinam.'

'Appane, I've met my share of liars. But not one of them can match your imagination and glibness.'

Vandiyadevan laughed to himself. What a fate he was doomed to! People were happy to believe his lies, but refused to believe the truths he told.

'Thambi, when did you leave Lanka?'

'Four days ago.'

'Ah, that is why you haven't heard the news yet.'

'What news, aiya?'

'That Ponniyin Selvar has drowned at sea.'

Vandiyadevan took great pains to act as if this came as a shock.

'Aiyo! Are you sure? Who told you?'

'There have been rumours about this since yesterday. Today, when the Pazhuvettaraiyar entourage passed his way, the village elders asked him. He confirmed that it was true. If only that paavi had been struck by lightning!'

'Why are you cursing that old man?'

'All this happened because of him. People are saying that he conspired to ensure that the prince drowned at sea. And so, they did away with all the arrangements they had made to welcome Pazhuvettaraiyar. How can we offer our respects to him after this? How can we treat him as a guest?'

'The villagers must adore the prince.'

'Need you ask? Everyone is in tears. And not just in this village. All of Chozha Naadu is in mourning. And everyone is cursing the Pazhuvettaraiyar brothers. The Chakravarti is already ill. How will this news hit him? Who knows what further debacles we have in store? The Dhoomketu has been spotted in the sky for a while now. It does portend something. Some awful event awaits us.'

Vandiyadevan ran through all the awful events that could unfold, in his mind. It struck him that it was a good thing the ironmonger had not believed him after all. He need not lie, but he could hide the truth of the prince. Ilaiya Piraatti must have had a crucial reason for sending him to the Choodamani Viharam. He would meet the prince, consult him on the course of action they should follow and act accordingly.

'Thambi! You seem to be lost in thought,' the ironmonger said. 'What are you thinking about?'

'I was caught at sea during the storm too. I escaped with my life by God's grace. I was thinking about that and thanking the Almighty.'

'Is there such a thing as God's grace?'

'Why do you say such a thing?'

'If there truly were such a thing as God's grace, would the Pazhuvettaraiyars still be able to carry out their evil plans? Would Ponniyin Selvar have drowned at sea?'

'Periyavare[4]! The Pazhuvettaraiyar brothers are in power and they wield great authority. How can you talk about them like this, with no thought of the consequences? What if someone were to overhear? Do be careful!'

'You're the one who should be careful, thambi, far more than I. At least I'm awake and fully conscious

when I speak. You speak in your sleep and blabber all
sorts of things.'

'Aiyo! What did I blabber?'

'You said the Pazhuvettaraiyar brothers are Yama's
henchmen. You referred to the Pazhuvoor Ilaiya
Rani as a malevolent spirit. Not that you're wrong,
of course. But what if someone other than I had
heard you? What would have become of you? And
at the very time you were saying all these things,
the Pazhuvettaraiyar entourage passed right by this
workshop. I was petrified.'

'What did you do?'

'I went outside as if I'd come to see the procession,
and locked the door of the workshop. Before that,
I made sure your horse was carefully hidden in the
backyard.'

'Did I blabber anything else?'

'Oh, there was no shortage of blabbering.'

'Aiyo! What else did I say?'

'You were pleading with the prince to come with
you to Pazhaiyarai. Apparently, he insisted that he
would do as the Pazhuvettaraiyar brothers wanted
and get arrested. And you went on and on, about a
whole lot of other things. Thambi! You even said all
sorts of things about Pazhaiyarai Ilaiya Piraatti. Careful,
appane, careful!'

Vandiyadevan hung his head in embarrassment.
What had he said about Ilaiya Piraatti? Had it been
something inappropriate, he wondered frantically.

From this day forward, he would only sleep alone, in a room the door of which he had fastened securely. Or in some isolated spot, like a forest or desert or mountain cave.

'Thambi! How did you get caught in the storm? And how did you escape?'

'The ship on which I was travelling was struck by lightning and began to sink. I kept myself afloat by holding on to the mast. And then, a boatwoman came that way and helped me get to shore.'

'Perhaps the prince, too, has survived, like you?'

'God willing.'

'Where did you stay last night?'

'I arrived in Kodikkarai, to find the Pazhuvettaraiyars had set up camp and occupied the entire place. So, I slept for a while at the Kuzhagar temple. And then I set off at dawn.'

'Ah, that is why you didn't hear the news about the prince.'

'Thank you for telling me, aiya. I must get to Pazhaiyarai now. And I should make sure I don't run into the Pazhuvettaraiyar entourage. Which way would be best?'

'Pazhuvettaraiyar is on the Rajpath to Thanjavur. If you stay by the riverbank and follow the river's course, you will get to Pazhaiyarai.'

'The sooner you have my horse shod, the better.'

'Almost done,' the ironmonger said, and took his hammer to the shoes he had been working in the furnace.

'There! This blow is for Periya Pazhuvettaraiyar! And this one for Chinna Pazhuvettaraiyar! And this one for Sambuvarayar! And this for Mazhavarayar!' he chanted, every time his hammer fell on the iron.

Vandiyadevan realised just how furious the people of Chozha Naadu were at the suzerain kings who had been part of the conspirators' group at the Kadambur palace.

The horse was shod before long.

Vandiyadevan took out some money for the ironmonger, but the man refused to accept it.

'I did this for you because you struck me as a fine young man. Not for money.'

Vandiyadevan thanked the ironmonger yet again, and took his leave.

Right as he was about to start riding, the ironmonger asked, 'Thambi, why are you going to Pazhaiyarai?'

'Aiya, if you don't ask me any questions, I won't have to tell you any lies,' Vandiyadevan said.

The ironmonger laughed, and said, 'What a quick wit you have! All it takes is a moment for you to make the switch. Just make sure you exercise such caution when you sleep too!'

When Vandiyadevan set off, it was nearly dusk. The sun had set before long, and darkness draped the world. Vandiyadevan had, nevertheless, managed to reach the riverbank. All he had to do was walk along it. There was no need to ask for directions.

It wasn't quite night, but millions of stars shone down on him. There weren't many trees lining the riverbank. The vegetation was mostly shrub. So, Vandiyadevan did not have to stumble around in the darkness cast by long shadows of the tree. He could see well by the light of the stars.

As if in competition with those stars, there were thousands of fireflies by the riverside. They flew in circles. Vandiyadevan's heart felt full. There were many reasons for his happiness. First, even as the entire kingdom was mourning the prince's death, Vandiyadevan alone was privy to the fact that he was safe. Moreover, he had seen for himself just how much the subjects loved their prince. He was also quite pleased by the fact that he had fooled Ravidasan a second time. But, more than anything else, it was the anticipation of his meeting with Kundavai Devi that gave him the most joy.

And he wasn't simply going to meet her, he was going to give her the news that his mission had been a triumph. He thought of all the obstacles he had overcome, and felt quite proud of himself. By this time tomorrow, he would have met Ilaiya Piraatti. Aha! Just the thought of it gave him gooseflesh.

The sky lit by stars, the earth glowing with fireflies, the bubble of the river, the gentle cooling breeze of the night, all gave Vandiyadevan the sense that the world and heavens had united to form a land of unadulterated joy. An old love song came to mind.

This was a rather appropriate place to let go and sing, he thought.

There was no sign of human life. Why, even the birds had gone to roost. Nothing would stop him from singing now. Here's how the song goes (and, of course, I need hardly tell you whom he was thinking of as he sang):

Vaana sudargalellaam
Maane undanai kandu
Meni silirkudadi; ange
Meimarandu nirkudadi!
Theno undan kuraldaan
Thenralo un vaai mozhigal
Meenotha vizhi malargal kandaal
Veri mayakkam taruvadeno?

All the stars in the sky
Glance at you, a gazelle,
And freeze, forgetting themselves,
Covered in gooseflesh from elation.
Honey is but your voice,
The gentle breeze but your words
Why do those fish-like eyes,[5]
Intoxicate one into stupor?

The moment Vandiyadevan began to sing, foxes set up a great howling in the distance. And, nearby, he heard a human laugh.

Startled, Vandiyadevan turned around quickly, and took a good look in every direction, even as he reached for his sword.

He spotted a figure under the dark shadows of a punnai tree.

'Thambi, what a fantastic song! And the foxes' song is even more fantastic!' the Devaraalan said, before collapsing into another fit of laughter.

13

THE POISONED POTION

Vandiyadevan's heart nearly stopped at the sight of the Devaraalan in that place, at that time. The memory of his frenzied dance and terrifying words at the Kadambur Palace came to mind, as did the words he and Ravidasan had spoken to him as the ship had bounced about the waves helplessly during the storm. It was hard to tell how much of that was true, and how much imagined. But he was certain of this much— they were involved in some sort of terrible secret conspiracy. Just his luck, Vandiyadevan thought, to have run into one of them in the middle of nowhere. He wondered for a moment whether he should simply make a run for it, urging his horse to fly. He looked about himself to gauge his prospects. He could see fire in the distance. It must be a crematorium.

A mortal body is now feeding that fire. When there was life in that body, how many ups and downs it must have seen! How many desires it must have been subject to, how many wishes must have tormented it! How many joys and how many sorrows it must have experienced! And yet, half a naazhigai will reduce all those desires and wishes and joys and sorrows into a fistful of ash. This is what will become of everyone born in this world. The grandest of kings and the poorest of paupers will one day turn into prey for this fire and end up as a fistful of ash, Vandiyadevan thought.

His panic disappeared as suddenly as it had set in. What reason did he have to be afraid of this trickster? Clearly, the Devaraalan was here to tell him something. He might as well hear it. Had it been the Devaraalan who had left by the backdoor as Vandiyadevan had entered the forge, he wondered. Perhaps that incredible sword had been his? Vandiyadevan was sure he had seen the insignia of a fish near the grip of that sword. He might be able to glean some information if he could draw the Devaraalan into conversation.

And so, Vandiyadevan set a leisurely pace for his horse. The animal, too, seemed to be struggling with his freshly-shod hooves. Vandiyadevan did not have the heart to urge the horse to go faster.

'How did you land up here, appa?' he asked.

'I should be the one asking that question,' the Devaraalan said. 'We left you on the ship in the middle of the sea, during a storm. How did you manage to escape?'

'You think you're the only one who knows mantras and magic? I'm not bad at it myself.'

'I'm glad to hear you believe in mantras and magic. I learnt from those very powers that you'd be wandering about all alone here. That's why I came ahead, to wait for you.'

'Why were you waiting? What business do you have with me?'

'Figure it out for yourself. Or, divine it with your magical powers.'

'You told me your secrets in the middle of the ocean. I don't know how much of what you said is fact and how much fiction. But I've decided to forget it all. I don't plan on telling anyone what you said.'

'I have no worries on that account. The moment you so much as consider telling a soul what we told you, your tongue will be sliced off. You'll end up mute.'

A chill ran down Vandiyadevan's spine. He thought of the two mute women he had met in Thanjavur and Lanka. He kept up a casual pace for some time. Why was this creature following him? How was he to lose the Devaraalan? If only he could find a pit of quicksand, as he had in Kodikkarai! Or, perhaps, he could throw the man into the river? No, there would be little point. The current wasn't too swift, and there wasn't enough water to drown him. Of course, if all else failed, he had his sword in his scabbard.

'Thambi, it's obvious to me what you're thinking. But it won't work. What's the point of undertaking a fool's mission?'

Vandiyadevan wanted to change the subject. He needed to buy some time to get away from the Devaraalan. It might be a good idea to taunt him into a useful revelation.

'What happened to your comrade, Ravidasan?'

The Devaraalan made a show of laughing and then said, 'You're the one who ought to know, right? Where is Ravidasan? You tell me.'

Vandiyadevan was startled. He ought not to have mentioned Ravidasan. He'd made a mistake. Had the Devaraalan met Ravidasan already, learnt what had passed and decided to put him to the test now, Vandiyadevan wondered. Or …

'Why, Thambi, why are you silent? Won't you tell me where Ravidasan is? Well, that's all right. At least tell me this … where is that boat-girl, Poonguzhali?'

At this, Vandiyadevan reacted like a man who'd just stepped on a snake. He was afraid to say any more.

'Oh, so you won't tell me about her either. Well, never mind. Perhaps you have a solid reason for wanting to protect her. Why, you were singing a love song some time ago, weren't you? Is she the one the song is in honour of?'

'No, no, I swear that's not true!' Vandiyadevan cried.

'Why are you so flustered? And so angry?'

'All right, all right, there's no time to talk about all that. Why have you caught my horse by his reins now? Let go! I need to leave, I'm on an important mission!'

'But you haven't asked me what *my* mission is.'

'How can I ask when you won't let me get a word in edgeways?'

'Well, you see, this Mullaiyaru shore has a unique power. If you make a wish standing here, it will be granted right away.'

'I have no wish or desire,' replied Vandiyadevan.

'That's a lie! The person whom you had in mind while singing your love song wishes to see you. If you'd like, you can meet her.'

'When?'

'Tonight.'

'What nonsense!'

'No nonsense, thambi. There, look!' and the Devaraalan pointed in the distance.

Vandiyadevan could make out a vague outline in the distance. He squinted. It was a palanquin, a closed palanquin.

Now, dear readers, where have we seen that palanquin before? Why, it is the Pazhuvoor Ilaiya Rani's palanquin, isn't it? Is Nandini inside, you wonder. As did Vandiyadevan. He couldn't contain his curiosity.

He sped towards the palanquin on his horse. He could see the curtain, and it seemed to him that someone parted it slightly from inside.

Vandiyadevan leapt off his horse.

At the same time, an odd sound emanated from the Devaraalan's throat.

From the bushes around him, bodies began to emerge. Seven or eight men closed in on Vandiyadevan and pounced on him and gripped him so tightly he could not so much as move. They bound his feet and hands, and then tied a blindfold over his eyes. One of them grabbed Vandiyadevan's sword. They then threw him into the palanquin. The palanquin began to move fast. The Devaraalan led the way, and the rest of the men followed, some carrying the palanquin and the others walking by it. One of the men led Vandiyadevan's horse.

All this had happened in a fraction of the blink of an eye. Vandiyadevan had been startled by the simultaneous attack from all sides. He could never have expected it. Now, sitting bound inside the palanquin, he could barely think. There was no way to figure out what the plan was. As they bounced him along though, his mind cleared slowly. The blindfold wasn't hard to dislodge. He manoeuvred his bound hands so he could part the curtain and look outside. They seemed to be taking a shortcut to somewhere, from near the riverbank.

It wouldn't be a hard task to free himself of the ropes that bound his hands and feet. It would then be easy to jump out of the palanquin, grab his horse and make a run for it. He could take on this lot, these seven—eight men who'd only been able to overpower him because of the surprise factor. He wondered if he should go for it. But something stopped him. There was some sort of obstacle.

The interior of the palanquin was perfumed by an ethereal essence. It was, at first, invigorating. He didn't have the heart to leave this scent behind just yet. It was too intoxicating. Where would the palanquin lead him? There was enough indication that it was Nandini who had sent for him. He did have a tiny little craving for just one more meeting with her ... and as time passed, that tiny little craving grew into an all-consuming ache. There were plenty of reasons he shouldn't give in to this desire. And yet, he found ways to rule out each reason, one by one. What could she do to him, anyway? Surely, it couldn't hurt to find out what it was she wanted with him? He might even learn something. He'd got himself out of every scrape in which he'd found himself thus far. Surely, he could counter any trap they set for him, and entrap his opponents instead? He was capable of that much, he knew it. There wasn't much chance he would see her again, after this. It was near impossible for him to go to Thanjavur. Simply too dangerous. Much easier to meet her en route. What harm could it possibly do him to meet the Ilaiya Rani, just once more?

Oh ... oh! And there was yet another crucial reason to meet Nandini. The Oomai Rani he had seen in Lanka! Was he right in his assessment that she resembled Nandini closely? He had to verify that, didn't he? He couldn't do that without another close look at the Pazhuvoor Ilaiya Rani's face, now, could he?

Even as these thoughts ran through Vandiyadevan's head, he began to feel lightheaded. Sleep weighed his eyelids down. No, no! This could not be sleep! He had slept almost through the day. No, this was something else, this was … the perfume in the palanquin was some sort of soporific, he thought. No, it was dangerous to stay on here! Aiyo! What peril! He would have to make a run for it!

Vandiyadevan began to undo the ropes that bound his hands. But … no, he couldn't. His fingers wouldn't move. He tried to sit up. He couldn't do that either. He tried to move his legs, but no … his limbs felt like they didn't belong to him anymore. His eyelids were closing. He couldn't think anymore. He was losing consciousness.

~*~

When Vandiyadevan came to, his instinct to jump out of the palanquin was strong. Yes, he could move now! He would jump … but … wonder of wonders! He was no longer in a palanquin. No, he was in an expansive room, brightly lit by the flame from many, many lamps.

This room was perfumed too. But it wasn't the same fragrance he had sensed inside the palanquin. This was heavy smoke, carrying the comforting smell of oil lamps. The old scent had dullened his senses, and this one heightened them. He sat up and took in his surroundings. A door across the room opened just then. Vandiyadevan waited eagerly to see who it was.

Nandini entered through the door. Vandiyadevan couldn't stop staring at her. There were many reasons for his fascination and astonishment. Her beauty, which defied all description, was one. The utter unexpectedness of this encounter was another. Yet another was the eerie resemblance between the faces and figures of the Oomai Rani from Lanka and this much younger woman. Was it only a resemblance? Or was one of them in disguise?

The Pazhuvoor Ilaiya Rani now smiled and said in a lilting voice, 'Aiya! You're a truly good man.'

'Vandanam[1]!' Vandiyadevan said.

'They say the hallmark of a good man is discretion. And you were so discreet that you disappeared from the palace without so much as a goodbye.'

Vandiyadevan laughed.

'I helped you enter the Thanjai palace. I gave you my signet ring. Surely, it would have been good form to return it to me before you left?'

Vandiyadevan was now embarrassed into silence.

'Surely, you can return it at least now, can't you? What use do you have for it? You can't have intentions of coming back to the Thanjavur palace, surely?' Nandini said, and extended an arm opening her palm, smooth and soft as a petal, for the ring.

'Devi! Senapati Boothi Vikrama Kesari confiscated the ring in Lanka. So, I find myself unable to return it to you. Please forgive me,' Vandiyadevan said.

'So, you've handed over the ring I gave you to my mortal enemy. What a show of gratitude!'

'I did not hand it over of my own free will. They forced it from my hands.'

'A scion of the Vaanar clan, the bravest of brave warriors descended from Vaanaathi Rayar, and you gave in to force? Unbelievable!'

'Ammani! I'm here right now by force, aren't I? Your men ...'

'Tell me the truth, aiya! Think back and answer honestly ... was it entirely by force that you were brought here? Was it not from your free will? Did you have no desire to see me? Did you have no opportunity to jump off the palanquin?'

Nandini's questions were as arrows that pierced Vandiyadevan's heart.

'Well, yes. I *am* here of my own free will.'

'To what end?'

'To what end did you have me escorted here?'

'To ask for my ring back.'

'Was that all?'

'There's another reason too. You were in the subterranean passage that night, weren't you? In the rooms that are part of the treasury that falls under my husband's charge?'

Vandiyadevan was startled.

'Did you think I didn't know? Could you have got away that night if it were not for me?'

'Devi …'

'Oh, yes, I know, I know it all. As does Periya Pazhuvettaraiyar. My husband ordered the guard to have you killed and your corpse disposed of right there. It was I who revoked the order when his back was turned. It is because of me that you got away, and your dear friend got into trouble instead. Otherwise, your bones would have been lying among those precious stones.'

Vandiyadevan was now swimming in a sea of surprise. He couldn't believe that she was telling the truth. But if she wasn't, how could she possibly know the details she did? Well, he supposed custom demanded that he thank her for saving his life. So, he began, 'Ammani …'

'No, please don't. I don't want you to say anything you don't feel. Please don't try to thank me when you feel no gratitude.'

'No, devi …'

'Do you know why I let you in on the fact that it was I who saved your life that day? Not from expectation of your gratitude, but to warn you not to use the subterranean passage any longer. It is heavily guarded now.'

'I have no plans of going anywhere near that place.'

'And why should you have such plans? It isn't in your nature to think of those who have helped you, is it? Your friend nearly lost his life because of you. It was I who had him brought to the palace, and I who nursed him back to health before sending him on his way. I hope it makes you happy to hear that? Or, is a penchant for betrayal of friendship inborn in you, along with your propensity for betrayal of trust?'

Nandini's words were as a poisoned potion that stuck in Vandiyadevan's throat and made his heart wilt. His silence came from suffering.

'You ensured the physician's son who accompanied you to Kodikkarai was arrested in your stead. Did you so much as enquire what became of him?'

'I intended to ask you.'

'I'll tell you. But you tell me first, what became of Prince Arulmozhi Varmar who accompanied you from Lanka? I'll tell you about the physician's son if you'll tell me about the prince.'

Vandiyadevan nearly jumped out of his skin. So, it was to learn what had happened to the prince that she had had him brought here. And that was why she had tormented him with her accusations. No, he must not allow her to find a chink in his armour. He would not succumb to her taunts.

'Arasi[2]! Please don't ask me about that one thing alone,' he said.

'Oh, of course! I shouldn't ask about that one thing alone! And even if I do, you won't respond. I know that. Well, am I allowed to ask what became of your lover girl? How is she doing? Would you be so kind as to share that with me?'

Vandiyadevan's eyes blazed. 'To whom are you referring? Careful!'

'Aha! I'm careful all right. Please don't think I'm referring to that Pazhaiyarai Maharani. She won't so much as spare you a second glance. You are as dust under her feet. I'm talking about the boatwoman who rowed you to and from Lanka. Isn't Poonguzhali your lover?'

'No, not at all! She introduced me to her lovers, in fact. She showed me the kolli vaai pisaasus that show up at midnight in the marshes of Kodikkarai, and told me those were her lovers.'

'What a lucky girl she is! Her lovers are creatures of light, who sparkle before one's eyes. My lovers, on the other hand, are creatures of the dark. They're shapeless and formless. Have you ever spent the darkest hours of the night in a desolate ruin? Have you heard the flapping of wings, and wondered whether the creatures flying about in the dark were bats or owls? My heart is one such desolate ruin, and my lovers are the creatures that fly within. They beat their wings and assault my chest. They brush their feathers against my cheeks. Where do those formless figures come from? And where are they headed? Why do they circle around me over and over again? Aiyo! Do you know?'

Nandini's haunted eyes looked wildly about the room as she spoke.

Vandiyadevan felt his heart melt. He felt unbearably sad. An overwhelming pity for this woman fought for primacy with an overpowering terror that he couldn't quite place.

'Devi! What is this? Calm down!' he said.

'Who do you think you are, to ask me to calm down?' Nandini demanded.

'I'm a poor young man born into the Vaanar clan. And who are you, devi?'

'Who am I? You ask who I am? I don't know who I am myself. I'm trying to find out. I'm trying to find myself. Are you asking whether I'm human, or a ghost or a ghoul?'

'No, no, I'm asking whether you're a divine being, perhaps an apsara, fallen from the celestial skies because of a curse, or ...'

'Yes! There is a curse upon me. I'm cursed! But I don't know what the curse is. I don't know who I am or what my purpose in life is. Why was I born? All I have is this little hint. Look! Here it is!' and with that, Nandini reached for a sword by her side.

It was newly forged. Its sharp point glinted in the light, and the reflection of the lamps bounced off the blade.

Vandiyadevan stared at the sword. He recognised it right away. This was the sword he had seen at the forgery. Thus far, Nandini's words had hit him like poison. Now, she had brandished a sword. Its iron gave him strength. His heart was fortified by the sight. He understood swords and spears. He had held them for as long as he could remember. He knew them, he had ties with them. He felt no fear of them. Nandini could use the sword against him for all he cared. He would feel no fear.

'Devi! I see it, I see the sword. I see the craftsmanship, and I know it is a royal sword. It is a sword that has been forged to be brandished by intrepid warriors. How did it make its way into your delicate hands? And of what is this a hint to you?' he asked.

14

FLYING HORSE

Nandini took the blazing sword and hugged it tight to
her chest. Then, she caressed her cheeks with it and
kissed the blade with her coral lips. It was like watching
a lotus kiss a ball of fire, Vandiyadevan thought. Or,
like a red cloud trying to hide the full moon.

The Pazhuvoor Rani's face had transformed. Now,
it appeared like that of the goddess Kali to whom the
Kapalikas[1] offered sacrifice. But the moment she kept
the sword back in its place, her countenance regained
its benign beauty.

'Yes, this sword is a hint, a sign that God has sent
me. But I do not know the import of it as yet. I have
it sent to the forgery every now and again to have
the rust removed and blade sharpened. I guard it like
a tigress does her cub. The cub shouldn't find itself
cornered by wild buffaloes before it is old enough to
look after itself, no? Have you seen how much love

the Arabs shower on their horses? I shower as much love on this sword.

'But God has not yet told me what I must do with it. Is it God's will that these hands, which have so far been used to make flower garlands, wield this sword and plunge the blade into the heart of an evil man? Or, that I sink it into my own heart so that blood bubbles over this body that is covered in silk and gold? I can't tell yet. I do have faith that the very God who has given me this sword will let me know what I must do with it when the time comes. However, since I don't know when that time will come, I am ready, day and night.

'Yes, it is true. The world believes that the Pazhuvoor Ilaiya Rani, who is synonymous with beauty, is obsessed with gold and silk and luxury. I spend all sixty naazhigais of every day anointing my skin with potions and hair with oil, indulging and pampering myself so I will forever epitomise beauty. My poor husband finds great joy in the belief that, in order to please him and to uphold his pride, I will forever shine in these ornaments. He has no clue of the fire that burns in my heart!'

Vandiyadevan, who had been listening to all this as if in a trance, suddenly came to himself and asked, 'Ammani! Where is Periya Pazhuvettaraiyar?'

'Why? Are you scared of that old man?' Nandini asked.

'No, ammani! I am not scared even of you, why would I be scared of Pazhuvettaraiyar?' Vandiyadevan said.

'Aha! This is why I like you. For some reason, everyone is scared of me. The greatest of heroes, the veteran of countless wars, the bearer of sixty-four scars on his body, Periya Pazhuvettaraiyar, is scared of me. Chinna Pazhuvettaraiyar—Kalantaka Kandar, who can make even time quake—trembles at the sight of me. The aspirant to the throne of the Chozha empire, Madurantaka Devar, is a mess of nerves whenever he comes to see me. Sundara Chozhar, who has one foot in the grave, turns pale and loses consciousness every time he sees me. As for Parthibendra Pallavan, who arrived today, and of whose fearlessness and valour I have heard tell, and whom I know to be Aditya Karikalar's closest confidante, took all of half a naazhigai to swear that he would serve me until his last breath. He has completely forgotten his duty to Aditya Karikalar, has forgotten that he was to rush to the crown prince the moment he landed in Kodikkarai and, instead, has been trailing me like a faithful pet. He will be happy to lay down his life to fulfil my smallest wish. And yet, when he approaches me, he is practically shaking. You know what this reminds me of? When I was a child, I used to like watching burning flames. I would go near the fire. I would reach out to touch the flames. But I couldn't muster the courage to actually put a finger to the fire. I would withdraw my hand at the last moment. I have done this many, many times. And when I see Parthibendran approach me eagerly and then hesitate, I'm reminded of my childhood proclivity for that pastime.

'Why single out Parthibendran? The very Aditya Karikalar whose trusted messenger you are is no different. We have known each other since we were children. His love for me knows no bounds; neither does his fear of me. What turns my life has taken because of this! Aiya! The next time you meet your master, would you convey a message to him from me? "I have buried all that happened in the past in the recesses of my memory. I am now the Pazhuvoor Rani and as a grandmother to Aditya Karikalar. There is no need to fear meeting me. I will not eat the crown prince up." Will you tell him this from me?'

'Devi! I cannot be certain that I will meet Aditya Karikalar alive. And even if I do, I have so much to tell him. I cannot be sure that I will remember to convey your message. Please do forgive me.'

'Of all the people I know, you're the only one I consider truly brave. You don't hesitate to speak your mind. What's in your heart is on your tongue. That is why I've grown fond of you. O Vaanar kula veera, valorous hero of the Vaanar clan! I do not meet many people. I don't ride a chariot like Pazhaiyarai Ilaiya Piraatti. Everywhere I go, I travel in a curtained palanquin. I only meet the people to whom I must assign tasks. Most of them are cowards. They don't dare tell me what is on their minds. You are not guilty of such pusillanimity or subterfuge.'

'I've realised there is no point in trying to hide anything from you, rani! No man can keep a secret that your eyes will not seek out and find in his heart.'

'That is perhaps true. But I'm not able to decipher what *your* heart holds. Well, that's as may be. You asked where my husband was. He and Parthibendran have gone with an entourage to a nearby village. A Kannagi Koothu[2] and Velanaattam[3] have been organised there. They've gone there to see if someone turns into an oracle in the frenzy of the dance and has some news to give about the prince. Madmen! They've let slip the man who can answer their questions, and turned to oracles and clairvoyants! They won't be back for a good while yet. That is why I sent for you. Aiya! I ask you again. You know the truth about the prince, don't you? But you won't tell me, will you?'

'No, devi! I cannot. I made a resolution, just today in fact, to never tell a lie again. And so, I cannot speak of the prince. I'm afraid I forgot this resolution some time ago. Please do forgive me,' Vandiyadevan said, and reached for the drawstring bag he had tucked into his waistband. He took out the ring with the palm insignia on it, and held it out. 'Ammani! Here is your signet ring. It is true that Boothi Vikrama Kesari's men had confiscated it from me. But the senapati returned the ring to me eventually. Here, I offer it back to you.

Please do me the honour of receiving it.' And with that, Vandiyadevan held out the ring.

Nandini stared at it, and verified for herself that it was indeed the ring she had given him.

'Aiya!' she said. 'It is not in my nature to take back what I give. I simply wanted to put your honesty to the test. You have passed with flying colours. You have not put me in a position where I'd be bound to ask my men to search you. Please do keep the ring in memory of me.'

'Ammani! Please give it some thought. If the ring remains with me, I will end up using it again to open doors for me.'

'I have no worries on that count. You may use it as you wish. I'm going to ask them to blindfold you again, and escort you in the palanquin to the spot from which you were picked up.'

'And if I refuse?'

'You won't be able to find your way out of this ruined palace and dilapidated fortress. You will find yourself going in circles.'

'Devi! This palace and fortress are ...'

'Once upon a time, Chozha Naadu was ruled by the Pallavas. For a very long time, in fact. The Pallava emperors built forts and palaces at this spot. Then, the region was claimed by the Pandiyas. They lived in this palace for some time. In the era of Vijayalaya Chozhar, there was a fierce battle. The fort was shelled. Half the palace was destroyed. We are now in the portion that was left intact. Some people refer to this as the Pallavarayan Fort, while others call it the Pandiyarayan Fort. There is truth in both. But it is only people who know their way here well who can get out of this place. So, what do you say? Should I ask my men to escort you? Or, will you make your way out by yourself and ...'

'No, devi! I don't have the time to waste on making my way out by myself. Let the men who brought me here escort me back. But before I go ... is this all you wanted from me? Is this why you had me brought here? Is there nothing else I can do for you? If you can think of anything at all, please don't hesitate.'

'Well, then. I'll tell you because you asked—I'd like a flying horse. If you can procure me one, please do come back to hand him over to me.'

'What? Did you just say "flying horse"?'

'Yes, a flying horse.'

'Are you referring to Arabian stallions that run so fast one could say they fly?'

'No, no! I could never mount such a horse. I am not talking about horses whose hooves touch the earth. I'm referring to an actual flying horse, one that will spread his wings like a bird and soar into the sky. I have heard stories of such horses in faraway lands. I want a flying horse, with wings!'

'And what use would you have for such a horse? Do you intend to fly to heaven?'

'Do I seem to you like someone who can find a place in heaven? I have not done the good deeds that would merit such a spot. I have committed many, many sins. I have done terrible things.'

'Have the residents of heaven not committed any sins? There are many who have fallen, and they have been sent to earth as punishment. Once they have done their penance and served their time, they return to heaven.'

'No, I have no interest in heaven. There is a desert in Pandiya Naadu. In the middle of the desert is a rock formation. Stones on which not even grass can grow, where not even weeds can thrive. There are some caves in this formation. Long ago, the Digambara sect of Jain monks would meditate in those caves. Now, snakes and foxes live there. I am fonder of these stones from Pandiya Naadu than of Amaravati in Devalokam.'

'Devi! You do have unique taste.'

'If I'm able to get hold of a flying horse, I will head to that desert. And then, I will fly to the island of Lanka from there. I have heard that there are mountains there that kiss the sky, and that the trees of the forests grow so tall they even hide the mountains from one's sight! That herds of elephant roam there, as common to spot as the herds of buffalo in Chozha Naadu. I will see all these sights.

'And I believe there are even greater wonders in other parts of the world. That there are mountains that were born on the day the world was born, whose slopes are white with ice, whose peaks shine like silver when the sun rises high. I wish to fly to the top of those peaks on this horse. And I've heard that there are deserts ten thousand times as large as that of Pandiya Naadu, where the sand is all white. In daytime, these deserts are so hot one feels that one is on fire. And that in lands farther away, the waters of the ocean have frozen from the cold and formed land masses firm enough for people and animals to walk on! I will go to all these places on my flying horse!'

'Devi! I'm afraid I can't bring you such a horse. However, it is quite simple to travel to some of the places you've mentioned. If you get on a well-fitted boat, it will take you barely half a day to reach Lanka. If you go by ship ...'

'Aiya! It is not that I'm unaware of such an option. But I'm scared of the ocean. I have a fear of ships. Why, I get scared even when the boat rocks gently on the ripples in the river! And so, your counsel is of little use to me. You may now take your leave,' Nandini said, getting up.

'Devi! Is there nothing else you wish to tell me?'

'No. But it seems to me that you wish to tell me something.'

'I wish to ask you a question. I pray that you will answer me. Were you not in Lanka some days ago? Did you not slip quietly by yourself among the shadows of the streets in Anuradhapuram?'

'No, not a chance. I have never stepped out of Pazhuvettaraiyar's palace without an escort. Why did you have such a suspicion?

'Ammani! I saw you some days ago in Lanka. You speak of flying horses. Perhaps you already have one, I thought, and perhaps you had flown to Lanka on that horse! But you were not wearing such grand silks and ornaments. Your sari was a simple one, and your hair was flying loose, unadorned. Was that lady not you?'

'No, not I, aiya! The woman you've mentioned ... did she say anything at all?'

'No, not in words. She spoke in signs. But you're acquainted with magicians. Perhaps you used some sort of sorcery to send a replica of yourself to Lanka, I thought.'

'And if it were not I or a replica?'

'It must be another woman, a woman who looks very much like you and does not have the gift of speech.'

Nandini was staring into the distance, lost in thought. She then let out a heavy sigh.

'Aiya! You said some time ago that you would be happy to help me, didn't you?'

'Indeed.'

'Did you mean it?'

'Most certainly.'

'In that case, give ear to this request. If you ever see that woman again, will you somehow bring her to me? Or, if you cannot do that, will you take me to her?' Nandini asked.

~*~

Within half a naazhigai, Vandiyadevan found himself at the same riverbank where he had been accosted. His horse was restored to him too. His escort vanished in a moment. The Devaraalan was nowhere to be seen, either.

He rode the horse through the night, sticking to the riverbank. During the third jaamam, a comet shot across the sky, tracing a vast arc. Vandiyadevan had often wondered whether the Dhoomaketu was indeed the portent of some disaster as people feared, or whether it was simply a blind superstition.

Every now and again, his mind wandered to Nandini. Her words were etched into his mind. The emotions she evoked in him had undergone a sea change. The disgust and hatred he had felt when he had first set eyes on her had now morphed into some sort of empathy, even pity. It was clear that she had been through some terrible trauma. But his tender feelings were peppered with some amount of anger at the fact that her true story remained a secret. Along with her unparallelled beauty, she carried something sinister too, some sort of power. And so, he thought, it was best to break off all ties with her.

If only she had accepted the ring! But she had refused. Of course, he could toss it into the river. But he couldn't bring himself to do that. It might come in handy when he next got himself into some sort of dangerous scrape. Why toss it away?

Once he had reached Pazhaiyarai and spoken to Ilaiya Piraatti, he would no longer have any use for it. He could throw the ring away then. He would never again step into this world of secrets and scrolls. No more annoying assignments, he decided.

During the fourth jaamam of the night, a spot of silver shone in the eastern sky. That was Shukra[4]. Vandiyadevan had heard that one must not continue a journey once Shukra had been spotted. And so, he stopped his horse and tied the animal to a tree. Then he lay down for a nap.

15

THE KALAMUKHAS

The red hands of the rising sun shook Vandiyadevan awake. But he wasn't quite in the mood to get up yet, and so he lay lolling about. He contrived to open his eyes and saw two figures in the distance. They had the appearance of ascetics, but not of the ordinary kind. They had a terrifying aspect. Their dreadlocks, the trishuls they bore and the fire pots they carried suggested they must be Veera Shaivites of the Kalamukha sect. What a pity Azhvarkadiyaan was not around to draw them into battle, Vandiyadevan thought. He decided he would pretend to be asleep until they had passed him by.

He sensed them stop by his side. He kept his eyes closed. One of the Kalamukhas came close and cleared his throat. Vandiyadevan remained motionless.

'Shivoham! The boy is Kumbhakarna incarnate,' the man said.

'Shivoham! How wonderful it would be if we could recruit a strapping young man like him!' his companion said.

'Shivoham! You've been fooled by his appearance. He's of no use to us, he will soon be subsumed by a terrible fate!' the first ascetic said.

It took his all for Vandiyadevan not to react to what he had heard. If he were to give in to his impulses and sit up, his bluff would be exposed. And then he wouldn't be able to hear the rest of their exchange. Perhaps they might say more about the terrible fate that lay in store for him?

However, that was not to be.

'Shivoham! It's his destiny, after all. Come, let's go,' one of the men said, and the two departed.

Vandiyadevan gave them some time to go on ahead, and then got up.

He will soon be subsumed by a terrible fate.

The words echoed in his ears.

~*~

The Kalamukhas had evolved from the Kapalika tradition. They did not offer human sacrifice like the latter, but that was the only real difference. Many believed that they could engage with the occult and tell the future. People also believed that they had the power to cast spells and curse those who fell foul of them. And so, everyone was keen to please them and oblige their requests, to ensure they did not fall prey to the anger of the Kalamukhas. The rulers of most minor kingdoms tended to set aside food for them at temples, and make funds available to them for their needs. However, the Chozha clan had so far done little by way of encouragement for the Kalamukhas.

Vandiyadevan, who was in the know of all this, decided to let them be. They were likely just making something up to frighten him. What peril could approach him that was greater than all that he had faced already?

He tried his best to persuade himself against making their acquaintance, but curiosity got the better of him. When he got to his feet, he saw the Kalamukhas walk past a ruin, not too far off. There was a manmade cave near the ruin, its entrance shaped like the roaring mouth of a lion. These caves had been built by the Digambara Jains, and were now being appropriated by the Kalamukhas.

Vandiyadevan was tempted to start a conversation with them. He left his horse behind, still tied to the tree, and made his way towards the cave. He could hear the men speak, from the other side of the rock.

'That boy wasn't putting on an act. He must have truly been asleep,' one said.

'How are you so sure of it?' the other asked.

'I'm yet to meet a man who is incurious once he's heard that a terrible fate awaits him,' the first said.

'There's something about him that suggests valour. Don't you think he would be a worthy recruit to our side?'

'What use do we have for young men like him? The emperor-in-waiting himself is all set to join the Kalamukhas.'

'To whom are you referring?'

'Who else, but Madurantaka Devan? Don't you know?'

'How is that possible? What about the other two in line to the throne?'

'One has apparently drowned at sea. The other's days are numbered.'

Vandiyadevan felt repelled by the conversation. He had no wish to continue listening to the men, let alone engage in dialogue with them. He simply wanted to get to Pazhaiyarai as soon as he could, speak to the princess and then leave for Kanchi. His primary allegiance was to Aditya Karikalar, after all. And the crown prince was surrounded by all manner of dangers. Now, Parthibendran, too, had fallen into the Pazhuvoor Ilaiya Rani's trap.

Aditya Karikalar was not given to thinking before he leapt into anything. Who knew what peril might find him? Vandiyadevan must rush to him and stand by his side to protect him. He shouldn't waste a moment on the way. He would leave right away.

Vandiyadevan made his way back to the horse silently. He jumped on the animal and spurred him on with a sharp tap to his side. When he passed the cave where the Kalamukhas were resting, he felt their eyes on him. He looked at them for a moment. One of the faces seemed familiar, but he didn't want to linger, and so he didn't give it more thought.

He passed several densely populated villages on his way. The news of the prince's death didn't seem to have reached them yet. The people of these villages were going about their daily tasks without a care in the world. Well, that was good, then. He must aim to reach Pazhaiyarai before the news preceded him. How would Ilaiya Piraatti feel if she heard that her brother had drowned? The princess might just hesitate to believe it, but what about the Kodumbalur princess? She could well die on the spot if she heard. The thought filled Vandiyadevan with a sense of urgency. But his horse was immune to that sentiment clearly, for the animal stumbled forward, unused to his newly-shod hooves. And so, it was nearly sunset before the outline of the Pazhaiyarai fortress appeared before Vandiyadevan.

The temple dedicated to Goddess Durga was visible near the entrance. But how would Vandiyadevan gain admission to the fortress? He had been coming up with various plots and discarding them all through the journey. The signet ring would be of no use here. The fortress guards would have been asked to arrest anyone who showed up with this ring. He would be sent straight to Chinna Pazhuvettaraiyar before he could speak a word to the princess, before he could even convey to her that he had arrived. He had no intention of letting that happen.

These thoughts had distracted him, and the horse took the opportunity to slow down. As Vandiyadevan was approaching the fort, he saw a group of men moving towards him. Men who were holding spears and shields, others on horseback ... and right in the middle, a golden chariot with the carriage in the shape of a lotus. Aha! Who was the occupant of the carriage? Surely, it was Prince Madurantaka Devar! The very same prince he had seen in the Kadambur Palace and in the subterranean treasury in Thanjavur! Vandiyadevan was inspired by a sudden idea—a way to get into the fortress!

'I'm yet to meet a man who is incurious once he's heard that a terrible fate awaits him.'

The words had been etched into his mind. He had failed to fight his own curiosity, hadn't he? This was a good time to put the Kalamukha's theory to the test.

Vandiyadevan spurred his horse on so that he surged towards the golden chariot at great speed.

Madurantaka Devar's entourage was entirely unprepared for this. The men were too surprised to stop Vandiyadevan, and his horse had reached the chariot before anyone had even realised what was happening.

Now, Vandiyadevan stood up on his horse's back, stared right into Madurantakar's eyes and hollered, 'O! Danger! Peril!'

Even as he said the words, he fell off his horse and rolled onto the ground. The horse bolted a few feet ahead from the momentum, and then came to a halt.

All this had occurred in the space of a few seconds. The soldiers, who had barely had time to react on seeing the approaching horse, were just about aiming their spears and reaching for their swords when Vandiyadevan slipped and fell, putting their minds at rest. This joker could cause no harm, surely!

Everyone looked at the man on the ground and began to laugh. Madurantakar joined them in mirth. His chariot had stopped. At a signal from him, two of his soldiers went up to Vandiyadevan to help him up. But the Vaanar scion had got to his feet before they reached him. He continued to stare at Madurantaka Devar, as if he had not just fallen off a horse and made a fool of himself.

'Bring the man here,' the prince said.

The two soldiers held Vandiyadevan by his arms and escorted him to the chariot. All through, he kept his stare fixed, looking right into Madurantakar's eyes.

'Appane ... who are you?' the prince asked.

'I ... I am me! Chakravarti Perumane![1] Do you not recognise me?' Vandiyadevan asked.

'What are you blabbering?' Madurantaka Devar said, and then ordered his men, 'Ade! Stand back.'

The soldiers glanced at one another and then moved out of earshot.

'Who did you think I was?' Madurantakar asked Vandiyadevan again.

'Forgive me, my prince! I have erred. You are not yet ... not yet ...,' Vandiyadevan made a show of fumbling.

'Have you seen me before?'

'Yes ... I have ... no, I haven't ...'

'Have you seen me or not? Tell me the truth!'

'I made a resolution, just yesterday, to never lie again. That's why I'm not able to tell you for sure,' Vandiyadevan said.

'Oho! So you're a truthful man as of yesterday? What kind of joke is this?' Madurantakar said, smiling. 'But why should that preclude your being sure whether or not you've seen me before?'

'What can one be sure of these days? Everyone looks like everyone else. Someone who rides in a closed palanquin one day appears in a golden chariot the next ...'

'What? What did you say?' Madurantakar asked, a tremor in his voice.

'Because everyone looks like everyone else, I can't be sure, I said.'

'And whom do I look like?'

'I've seen you twice before. Or I've seen someone who looks like you twice. I can't be sure, as I said.

And it was only to ascertain for myself that I … uh, sometime ago … uh …'

'Stood on your horse's back and stared at me?'

'Yes, aiya!'

'And what did you learn?'

'It could be you that I saw. Then again, it might not be. That's what I learned.'

Madurantakar's expression and tone betrayed his annoyance. 'You're a rascal. I'm going to …'

'Please, prince, don't be angry. I'll tell you where I saw you, or your lookalike. And then, you can decide what I am and what you should do with me.'

'Well, tell me then, quick!'

'A large fortress with high walls on all four sides. There were several great warriors present in a hall. It was midnight, a secret conference. They spoke in angry voices, in the dim light cast by a lamp hanging from a nook in the wall. There was a palanquin in one corner of the room. One of the warriors was being bombarded with questions by everyone else. He then pulled open the silk curtain that was drawn across the palanquin. A man who was the very epitome of beauty stepped out of the palanquin. The moment they set eyes on him, the other warriors began to cheer. "Vaazhga! Vaazhga! Long live! Long live!" they cried. Some shouted, "Long live the crown prince!" I even remember some saying, "Victory to the emperor!" Aiya, the face of the man who stepped out of the palanquin was quite like yours. But if I've said anything I ought not to have, please do forgive me.'

Madurantaka Devar had been listening silently all this while. Now, beads of sweat appeared on his brow. His face was pale, fear writ on every contour.

'O Truthful-One-as-of-yesterday! Were you among those warriors?'

'No, aiya, I promise I was not.'

'Then how do you recount these events as if you had witnessed them?'

'I'm not sure whether the incident truly occurred or whether I saw it in a dream. Listen to this other vision I had too. A subterranean passage winds through a cavernous palace. Three people are walking through it, climbing up and down flights of stairs. A man walks ahead, holding a torch. A bodyguard walks behind them all. And between them is a man who is as handsome as Manmadha, a prince among men. As the flame from the torch lights the way, one can see the light bounce off gold and gems and precious ornaments along the way. It appears to be some sort of secret treasury, where treasures from various kingdoms have been stowed away. The pillars are sculpted with demonic faces. The face of the handsome man in the middle resembled yours. It is you who must confirm whether this was true or not.'

'Enough, stop it!' Madurantakar cried, his voice shaking with fear.

Vandiyadevan fell silent.

'Are you a nimithakaaran?[2]'

'No, aiya, that is not my profession. But I can tell you the past, and I can tell you the future.'

Madurantakar thought for some time and then said, 'You shouted something to me while standing on the horse. What did you say?'

'I said, "O danger! Peril!"'

'Who is in danger?'

'You!'

'What kind of danger?'

'You're surrounded by all manner of danger. And there is great fortune waiting for you too. It will take me some time to explain. But your soldiers have divested me of even my sword. If I could be permitted to enter the fortress with you ...'

'Certainly. Come with me. We will talk at leisure!'

Madurantaka Devar gestured to the leader of his squad. He ordered that Vandiyadevan be escorted into the palace. The soldier did not appear pleased by this, but he didn't have a choice. He stood by Vandiyadevan's side and accompanied him, his teeth gritted the whole time.

Soon, the gates of the fortress opened. Madurantakar and his entourage entered, Vandiyadevan in their midst.

16

MADURANTAKA DEVAR

We've met one of the most important characters of this story, Madurantaka Devar, twice already. We saw him early on, in the Kadambur palace. Later, we encountered him passing through the subterranean passage at the Pazhuvettaraiyar palace in Thanjavur. However, this prince who had already gained such fame, and who will one day sit on the throne of the Chozha empire with the title Parakesari Uttama Chozhar, has not been properly introduced to our readers. That oversight must be set right here.

Before we get into the details of Madurantakar's life, the readers should perhaps have at the ready a little reminder of his progenitors. Before Sundara Chozhar, the emperor who had ruled for a considerable period of time was his uncle—Madurantakan's father— Kandaraditya Chozhar. This emperor and his wife, the daughter of Mazhuvarayar, Sembiyan Mahadevi, were exemplary devotees of Shiva. They had dedicated their lives to worship and to the renovation of Shiva temples.

Kandaradityar had longed to have all the Devaratirupadigams[1], which were scattered across Tamizhagam, compiled. This did not happen in his lifetime. But he did manage to collect some of these padigams, and added some of his own verses too. One of the verses he composed about Chidambaram still finds a place in the *Tiruvisaippaa*.[2]

The verse speaks of Parantaka Chakravarti's endowment of a golden casing for the Tillaiambalam, or roof of the inner sanctum of the temple there.

It goes:

Vengol vendan thennannaadum
Eezhamum konda tiral
Sengol chozhan kozhivendan
Sembiyan ponnaninda
Angolvalaiyar paadi aadum
Mani tillaiambalaththul
Engol eesan empiraiyai enru
Kol eidhuvathe!

The king who has conquered
The southern lands and Eezham
The Chozhan who wields the sceptre
Kozhivendan as he is known
Has graced Tillai Ambalam with Sembiyan gold[3]
So everyone may sing and dance with joy
In the worship of our lord Shiva!

In this verse, he praises Parantaka Chozhar as the ruler of Pandiya Naadu and Lanka (Eezham). In the last verse of this padigam, he mentions his own name and says the capital of Chozha Naadu was Thanjavur under his rule:

Seeranmalgu tillai semponnambalaththaadi thannai
Kaaraar cholai kozhivendan thanjaiyar konkalanda
Aaraavin sol Kandaradityan aruntamizh maalai vallaar
Peravulagil perumaiyodum perinbam eithuvaare!

Of the Tillaiambalam encased in Sembiyan gold,
The king of Uraiyur and Thanjavur, the Kozhivendan
Who rules a land with bowers and gardens buzzing
with bees
So many as to give the impression of a rain-bearing
cloud,
Has sung praise written in verse inspired by the lord.
Those who sing these beautiful Tamil words, knowing
their import,
Will never return to the earth once they ascend to heaven,
And will find great joy and be the subjects of great
respect for eternity!

Kandaradityar had little interest in expanding his empire by waging war. He was moved by the suffering of people in wartime, and did his best to avoid subjecting them to it. In spirit, he embraced the tenets of Jainism even while remaining a Shaivite. And so, the empire had shrunk in size during his time. He married the daughter of Mazhuvarayar in his twilight years, and had a son who was but an infant even as the father approached dotage. All this while, enemies were at the gates, salivating.

It was a fraught time. Kandaradityar's brother Arinjayan had been severely wounded in war and was on his deathbed. However, the latter's son Sundara Chozhar won practically every war he fought. His victories had already earned the young prince a reputation as a dauntless warrior and astute general. So, Kandaradityar decided that it was Sundara Chozhar who should inherit the kingdom after him, and held a ceremony to announce this to the people. In order to ensure that there was no infighting in later generations, he also announced that Sundara Chozhar's progeny would be the rightful heirs to the Chozha throne.

He had already told his wife that their son must be raised as a devotee of Shiva, and dedicate his life to austerity and worship. The entire kingdom was aware of this, and Sembiyan Mahadevi kept the promise she had made to her husband. She instilled in her son the tenets of Shaivism and emphasised the importance of renouncing worldly life and devoting oneself to worship right from when Madurantakan was a toddler.

For about twenty years, the prince treated his mother's words as scripture. He had no interest in governance. It never even struck him that he was entitled to the Chozha throne. However, after marrying Chinna Pazhuvettaraiyar's daughter, something changed in him. The thought that he was the rightful heir to the throne occurred to him, and the Pazhuvoor Ilaiya Rani fanned the flames of this desire. Soon, it raged inside him with the intensity of a forest fire.

As we already know, several suzerain kings and veteran warriors had thrown in their lot with Madurantakar, all to serve their own vested interests. They were waiting for Sundara Chozhar to die so that they could crown his cousin king. However, Madurantakar was not of a mind to wait until the emperor's death. He felt he had been cheated out of his inheritance. Sundara Chozhar had no right to the throne. And now, he was too ill to run the empire. So, why was he not being crowned king already to take his place and bring governance to the land?

It was no mean task for the Pazhuvettaraiyar brothers to keep Madurantakar's newfound ambitions in check. They didn't want him to ruin it all in his haste. Sundara Chozhar's two sons were fearless, astute, supremely skilled warriors whose various feats and character traits had won them great love from the people of the land. They had Kodumbalur Velaar and Tirukkovalur Malayaman by their side too. Most of the emperor's army was loyal to his sons and intended to serve one of the princes if they had the chance. And so, the Pazhuvettaraiyar brothers knew it would be most prudent to wait until the emperor had died.

If they could get Sundara Chozhar to declare that the throne should go to Madurantaka Devar after him, there would be no problem at all. The only obstacles to this were Ilaiya Piraatti Kundavai Devi and Periya Piraatti Sembiyan Mahadevi. The former's ploys could be countered easily enough. But if Sembiyan Mahadevi, who was seen by the entire empire as divinity itself, objected to this, there was little they could do. Word had already got around that she had no wish for her son to rule the empire. How would the subjects accept as king a man who did not respect his mother's wishes? It would be most convenient if she followed her husband to Kailash, of course. But since she showed no signs of dying anytime soon, the only option they had was to change her mind. And who was better equipped to change a mother's mind than the son she had borne?

So, the Pazhuvettaraiyar brothers took every opportunity they got to urge Madurantakar to confront his mother and persuade her that the Chozha throne must go to him. He was burning to take over the reins of the empire. But he baulked at the idea of speaking to his mother about it. These days, he hesitated to speak to her about anything at all, for that matter.

Now, Periya Piraatti herself had sent word to Thanjavur that she wanted to make an announcement regarding the fulfilment of one of her husband's greatest wishes, and that her son must be by her side as she announced it. Chinna Pazhuvettaraiyar was obliged to ask Madurantakar to head to Pazhaiyarai. He also urged his son-in-law, yet again, to speak to his mother about his right to the Chozha throne.

17

TIRUNAARAIYUR NAMBI

Madurantaka Devar entered the walled city of Pazhaiyarai along with his entourage and Vandiyadevan. Their procession passed the quarters that were reserved for the army and their families—Arya Padai Veedu, Pambai Padai Veedu, Puduppadai Veedu, Manappadai Veedu and so on. Then came the streets with the shops, the residential areas, the temples and the streets where the priests who served the temple lived.

Every now and again, they came across a family that was waiting for a procession, but most of the people didn't seem in any way excited or inspired by the sight of Madurantaka Devar. The first time Vandiyadevan had visited Pazhaiyarai, the streets had been teeming with people. Now, they were empty. One might even wonder whether the town had been deserted for some reason. It was clear as day that no one cared much for Madurantakar. Their lack of interest in the procession suited Vandiyadevan. For, as long as the streets were empty, there was less chance of someone recognising him.

As they were approaching the street where the royal palaces were, they saw a procession approaching from the opposite direction. In the middle was an open palanquin. It wasn't quite clear who the occupant was, but his appearance suggested he was a devotee of Shiva and very young. People crowded around the palanquin. Some sang, while some kept time with cymbals.

Cheers of 'Tiruchitrambalam!', 'Hara hara Mahadeva!' and 'Tirunaaraiyur Nambi Vaazhga!' rose from the crowd. Some cried, 'Pollaa Pillaiyarin Arutchelvar Vaazhga! Long live the beloved son of Pollaa Pillaiyar!'[1]

Madurantakar looked at the procession with some envy. He posed a question to the soldier by his side, who replied, 'Yes, it is indeed Tirunaaraiyur Nambi!'

'But what a fuss these people are making! No one cares about me, but how they swarm around this Nambi fellow!' Madurantaka Devar said.

They were still some distance away from the other procession, but Vandiyadevan thought he spotted in the crowd the Veera Shaivite who had got into a quarrel with Azhvarkadiyaan while crossing the Kollidam by boat.

The entourage entered the royal complex and wound its way to Sembiyan Mahadevi's palace. Periya Piraatti was waiting outside the palace, anxiously looking for someone.

Touched by his mother's concern, Madurantakar dismounted from his chariot and bowed before her. She planted a quick kiss on the top of his head and said, 'My dear son, I'm glad you're here. Tirunaaraiyur Nambi is on his way. If you must, go to your quarters to freshen up, but make sure you don't take too long to come to the sabha mandapam!'

Vandiyadevan observed the glow dissipate from Madurantaka Devar's face. The poor man must have thought his mother was waiting to welcome him, only to find she was waiting for the Shiva devotee arriving in a grand procession. Here was her only son, who considered himself the rightful heir to the Chozha throne, and all she cared about was a young ascetic?

They repaired to Madurantaka Devar's chambers. He took his time washing himself and changing his clothes. He seemed in no hurry to head to the sabha mandapam. Messenger after messenger arrived from his mother, urging him to hurry, until he finally relented.

As he was leaving, he said, 'Where is the nimithakaaran?'

Vandiyadevan, who was aching to accompany him to the sabha mandapam, cried, 'Here I am! I'm ready!'

Madurantakar made for the sabha mandapam with a small escort that included Vandiyadevan.

An assembly had already gathered at the sabha mandapam. On one side sat Sembiyan Mahadevi, Ilaiya Piraatti Kundavai Devi and some other women from the royal family. Right at the centre of the hall, on a regal platform built for the purpose, sat a young man. He wore rudraksha beads and had vibhuti smeared on his forehead and arms. His face shone with natural radiance. Before him were a pile of scrolls. He had one in his hands too. Beside him stood an elderly man, also wearing rudraksha beads and vibhuti. The people of Pazhaiyarai had gathered in large numbers.

Vandiyadevan ascertained that the young man before him had been the one in the palanquin, and that the elderly man by his side was the Shaivite from Kollidam. His eyes took in everything in the sabha mandapam, but wandered over and over again to the beloved face next to Periya Piraatti's, that of Kundavai Devi. As for the princess, her eyes had betrayed her surprise for a fraction of a second when she had first laid eyes on him, but she determinedly kept her gaze elsewhere thereafter. She ignored him so completely that he wondered whether she had failed to recognise him after all.

The moment Madurantakar entered the sabha mandapam, all those gathered there except for the royal women rose to their feet and bowed. The moment he took his seat, everyone else sat down too.

His mother turned to him and said, 'Kumara! This young man is from Tirunaaraiyur. He has been blessed by the Pollaa Pillaiyar of that town. He has got his hands on some Devara padigams which no one else has found before. Long ago, a princess named Mangayarkarasi from our Chozha dynasty became the maharani of Pandiya Naadu. At her behest, Aaludaiya Pillaiyar Gnanasambandar[2] went to Madurai. He held a debate with the Jain scholars there and was declared the winner. This young man has found the padigams that Sambanda Swami sang at the time in Madurai. Some of these are in praise of the maharani too. When I hear these songs, I feel bliss in every pore of my body. If only your father had been here to listen to them, how joyful he would have been! You must listen in his stead!'

'I will, thaaye. May the recitation begin!' Madurantakar said.

But his face remained dull, as if his heart was not in this at all. He was not happy about everyone dancing attendance on the young man with his rudraksha beads and vibhuti. He was simply indulging his mother by calling for the recitation.

Tirunaaraiyur Nambi began to read from the scroll in his hands. He began with the song Gnanasambandar had sung the moment he had entered Madurai, praising the city in which the epitome of devotion to Shiva, the queen Mangaiyarkarasi, lived.

Mangaiyarkarasi valavarkon paavai
Varivalai kaimadamaani
Pangayaselvi pandima devi
Paniseithu naadorum parava
Pongazhaluruvan bhoota naayaganal
Vedamum porulgalum aruli

Angayarkanni thannodum amarntha
Aalavaayaavadum iduve!

Mangaiyarkarasi, daughter of our emperor,
Who wears striped bangles on her arms,
Her naivete so becoming of femininity,
Incarnate of the goddess who sits on the lotus.
She who worships the lord all day,
Graced with knowledge of the words and meaning
Of all four vedas, is pure as the fire of Shiva himself.
She rules over this glorious city whose temple
Is ruled by Shiva with his consort Angayarkanni![3]

Mannellaam nigazha mannanaal mannum
Manimudi chozhanranmagalaam
Panniner mozhiyaal pandima devi
Paanginaarpani seithu parava
Vinnulor iruvar keezhodumelum
Alapparidaam vagai ninra
Annalaar umaiyodu inburuginra
Aalavaayaavadum iduve!

Queen to the king who rules the entire world,
Daughter of the Chozha emperor
Who wears the bejewelled crown
The Mahadevi of Pandiya Naadu,
Whose words are song,
Whose devotion is unmatched,
She rules over this glorious city,

Where the lord rejoices alongside
All those who people the three worlds!

As she heard these words, tears of joy fell as pearls from Sembiyan Mahadevi's eyes. It struck her that she must have earned great punyam in her previous births to have married into the clan that had produced such a great devotee and such an inspiring scholar as Mangaiyarkarasi.

Madurantakar for his part could only think about the phrase 'The Chozha emperor who wears the bejewelled crown'. That crown ought to have been his. It was his birthright. And yet, someone else was wearing it at this moment. It filled him with rage and frustration to think of it.

Nambi had moved on to the next song. He recounted the moment when Gnanasambandar went to meet Mangaiyarkarasi. The queen looked at him with concern. He was so young, she thought, so young that when he spoke, the smell of breastmilk emanated from his lips.[4] The Jain scholars would eat him alive, she thought. Sensing what was going through her mind, Gnanasambandar sang:

Maanin nervizhi maadaraai, vazhudikku
Maaperundevi kel!
Paanalvaai oru baalan ingeevan
Enru nee parivu eithidel!
Aanai maamalai yaadiyaaya
Idangalirpala allal ser

Eenargatkeliyen alen tiru
Aalavaayaran nirkave!

O lady with the eyes of a deer,
Queen to the Pandiya king, listen!
Do not worry that a boy so young
Stands before you to debate.
I am not any less competent
Than the men from Aanaimalai and elsewhere
The Jain scholars who inflict suffering
On the people of those regions.
For I am blessed by the grace
Of the Lord Aalavaayaran![5]

As Tirunaaraiyur Nambi sang those lines, Sembiyan Mahadevi could see herself as Mangaiyarkarasi and the young man before her as Gnanasambandar. She found herself in a trance, living in another world.

As for Madurantaka Devar, he was thinking, *Yes, I am young, a mere boy before the emperor. But I am no less competent that Tirukkovalur Malayaman and Kodumbalur Boothi Vikrama Kesari and Sundara Chozhar to whom they are so loyal! Just as Aalavaayaran blessed Gnanasambandar with his grace, the Pazhuvettaraiyar brothers have chosen to stand by my side!*

Vandiyadevan did not even register the words. His eyes and mind were entirely on Kundavai Devi. Had the princess truly failed to recognise him? Or was she pretending she hadn't? Or, was she angry that he had not rushed to her right away with his report? His mind was besieged by these thoughts. He was also wondering what ruse he would use to meet Ilaiya Piraatti in private, and how he would break the news of Ponniyin Selvar's illness to her.

Once Nambi had finished singing, Sembiyan Mahadevi turned to the older man who had accompanied him and said, 'Aiya! When I look at this little boy, I feel I'm looking at Gnanasambandar himself! He must be a reincarnation of the great saint. You must take him to every village and town and city in Tamizhagam! You must collect the Devaram verses you find in each one of those places. Separate compilations must be made of verses by Appar, Sambandar and Sundaramurty. These verses must be sung every day in every Shiva temple in this land. This was my late husband's wish. It is my deepest desire to fulfil that wish in my lifetime. Everything you need for this undertaking will be provided for by the royal family— your palanquins, entourage and anything else. I will send my son as messenger to the emperor, carrying this request from me!'

The cheers and applause that rose from the assembly fell as an assault on Madurantakar's ears.

18

THE NIMITHAKAARAN

Once the assembly began to disperse, Periya Piraatti turned to her son and said, 'My boy, I'm going to see them off at the palace gates. In the meantime, go to your room, get refreshed and come back. There's something important I have to discuss with you.'

'As you wish, thaaye,' Madurantakar said, and left for his quarters.

Rage and envy burned in his chest. What a fuss his mother had made over a couple of medicants! The entire Chozha clan would become laughing stock thanks to his mother, he thought. She was making a mockery of royalty itself. No wonder the Pazhuvettaraiyar brothers found fault with his mother so often. All one needed to do was appear before her with rudraksha beads and ash smeared on one's body and sing a padigam he claimed to have found, or blather on about temples and holy dips and service to the lord, and she would empty out the treasury for them. As if that weren't enough, the princess Kundavai Devi was constantly by her side, waiting for leftovers. If Periya Piraatti forgot a chest or two in the treasury, Ilaiya Piraatti would donate it to the aadurasalai in one temple or another. If these women were allowed to do whatever they wanted, what would be left in the royal treasury when he ascended the throne? He dreamt of sending out armies in every direction to wage wars and conquer kingdoms and expand the Chozha empire. How would this ever come true if he could not fund such an enterprise?

And now, his mother wanted yet another private audience with him! Who knew what she was going to say? She would probably go on about ashtanga yoga or nididhyasana! She would ponder about whether if one focused hard enough on kundalini yoga, hard enough to go cross-eyed, one would be able to learn all the sixty-four ancient Tamil arts without studying any. Or she would want to analyse the deeper meaning of Nataraja's dance of bliss. What could his flowing hair signify, she would wonder, and what about the crescent moon that adorned it? It was two decades of internalising all this rubbish that had brought him to a state where the world considered him half-mad. No, he would not give her place to fill his mind with all this nonsense from here on out. Even if she insisted on speaking to him, he would make sure he didn't listen, even as he heard the words.

Well, that's as may be. Before his mother started badgering him with messengers, he must speak to the nimithakaaran. How had he learnt two secrets to which he could not possibly be privy? Madurantakan had been shocked by it. Surely, the man must have formidable powers of magic! If he could see the past so clearly, perhaps he could see the future too? He must meet him and find out.

He had noticed the nimithakaaran looking about himself and lingering on when they were leaving the sabha. He had gestured to the man to accompany him.

~*~

Vandiyadevan had been hoping to catch the princess's eye, and convey that he would like to meet her. But she had not so much as glanced in his direction, and had left the sabha with Sembiyan Mahadevi.

What was the meaning of all this? Had the princess truly forgotten him? That must be the case. She met thousands upon thousands of people every day. How would she remember a face she had seen only a couple of times?

Vandiyadevan told himself he was a madman. He had played the princess's face before his mind's eye a million times a day, through all the peril he had encountered, through all the events that had occurred on his journey. But what reason could the princess have to think of him? A bee buzzed around the flower, desiring its nectar. The flower, however, did not care for the bee. The flower only smiled at the sun. Who was the sun who made the princess's face blossom with joy?

So, she might not care much for him, but surely she must be keen to find out what had happened in Lanka? Or could news of this have reached her already? How was that even possible? No, no! Her expression had betrayed her anxiety. The only explanation for her behaviour was that she had failed to recognise him. She could not be expected to guess that the messenger tasked with carrying her secret scroll to Lanka should appear in Madurantaka Devar's entourage. How surprised she would be when he told her about his ploy to gain entry into the palace! But how would he tell her? How would he meet her? How would ...?

'Nimithakaara! You seem to be deep in thought,' Madurantakar said.

Vandiyadevan came to with a start.

They had reached Madurantakar's quarters by now.

Back in the day, there were various kinds of men who were empowered to tell the future—astrologers or josiars, horary astrologers or aaroodakaarars, palmists or regai josiars, and nimithakaarars. Josiars specialised in reading horoscopes and studying astronomical charts to predict the future. Aaroodakaarars made a horoscope based on a question that was posed and the time at which it was posed, and various factors that governed the people and the motives involved.

Palmistry continues to this day, and so one needs little explanation.

Nimithakaarars were men who had some sort of extra-sensory perception. They had trained their minds to focus on the past and the future so that they could have visions of incidents as if they were happening right before their eyes. Some would close their eyes and meditate in order to focus. Others would stare at a flame which would turn into a screen to their eyes and play out the past and future. Still others could divine the past and future of a person simply by looking at his or her face.

And then there were the more ordinary nimithakaarars, nowhere near as skilled as the men of whom we have spoken. They would look at omens such as the direction in which a crow had flown and assign significance to such mundane events.

When Madurantakar called out to him, Vandiyadevan was startled. He remembered he had to play the role of nimithakaaran, but he couldn't tell what questions the prince might pose to him. He must make sure he handled them without getting himself into any trouble. Good god, he thought, how was he going to get away from this place and this man? How was he going to meet the princess?

'Oh, nothing much, aiya. It struck me that if only I had, instead of being a nimithakaaran, learnt a few padigams like that boy who was honoured at the sabha, how much fuss would be made over me, how regally I would be treated!'

'Who's stopping you? Why don't you learn a few Devara padigams and land up here?'

'Well, one's destiny has been preordained, hasn't it, ilavarase? What's the point of wishing it were otherwise?'

'What did you think of that boy who sang padigams? What do you think his future might be?'

'An extremely bright one. He is destined to be smiled upon by both the divine and the royal. Great emperors and empresses will seek his blessings, and honour him in their courts. His name will be written into history alongside those of great saints.'

Vandiyadevan spoke those words without thinking. He had simply said what came to his mind at that moment.

However, his words left Madurantakar's mind in great turmoil.

'And what does *my* future hold?'

'Yours is quite like his. The divine and the royal smile upon you. But you will reach even greater heights!'

'Appane, tell me in more detail.'

Vandiyadevan needed to buy some time. He thought quickly, and then said, 'How can you be in such a hurry? These things need patience. We must light a lamp. Then, you must sit before the flame. I will watch the scenes play out, and then tell you the details you want to know.'

Madurantakar hastily sent his men to arrange for a lamp to be lit. Two wooden platforms were placed on either side of the flame, for the two men to sit. Once Madurantakar had taken his seat, Vandiyadevan sat down too.

He closed his eyes and appeared to be deep in meditation. His mouth moved, as he mumbled a series of chants. Then, he began to shake as if he were being possessed. Suddenly, he opened his eyes wide and stared straight ahead. He looked into the flame, and then turned to Madurantaka Devar and said, 'Aiya! Please forgive me if I have said something that is not quite right. Your future is no ordinary one. It is nothing like that of the boy who sang in the sabha. His future is bright thanks to the royalty with whom he finds favour. But what I see about you in the flame … aha! I can barely believe it?'

'What do you see? Tell me! Tell me!' Madurantakar breathed.

'Aha! But how will I tell you? How will I find the words? For as far as the eyes can see, kings wearing bejewelled crowns stand in line. Ministers and warriors and leaders of men wait in attention, while just beyond is a sea of men, an army greater than anyone could envision! Their spears and swords and armour shine like gold. People crowd on to the terraces of buildings and cheer for you! Why, some of them have even climbed the ramparts to look at you. They're … they're saying something.'

'What are they saying? Tell me!'

'There are so many voices shouting all at the same time that I'm not able to hear the words clearly. Thousands of people cheering! They seem to be saying the usual things, "Chozha kula thondral vaazhga! Tribhuvana Chakravarti vaazhga! Mannaadi mannar vaazhga! Long live the Chozha scion! Long live the emperor of the three worlds! Long live the greatest of kings!"'

'And then?'

'The people are surging forward like waves in the sea. The soldiers block their way. For a while, there is great commotion.'

'All right, all right. But why has the crowd gathered? What is the occasion?'

'I'm waiting to see that. I can see the tiger flag flying so high it grazes the sky. Below it are flags bearing various emblems—fish, palm tree, bow, lion, bull, boar ... And in the middle of the sabha is a throne of gold with precious stones embedded in it. On a decorative platform by it is a crown studded with invaluable gems. Ah, it shines like a thousand suns! A large umbrella of white silk has been spread above the throne. Women who look like apsaras hold white chamaras[1], waiting for the occupant of the throne. Water from various holy places has been gathered in a row of golden pots. Ilavarase! It seems to be the pattabhishekam ceremony. The coronation of the new king.'

'Whose coronation is it? Tell me that, appane!' Madurantakar said.

'We'll know shortly. The outer doors of the sabha have just been flung open. Criers are entering, calling out all sorts of cheers. Behind them is an old man of regal bearing and enormous stature, a man who has seen many wars. He is followed by another man, who appears to be his brother. They are followed by a prince so handsome he could be Manmadha himself!'

'Who is that? Who is that?'

Vandiyadevan stared at Madurantakar's face, and then turned back to the lamp.

'Aiya! He looks just like you! Well, not like you … he *is* you! The two men who preceded you are escorting you to the throne. Cries of "Jaya vijayibhava!" rise from the crowd, louder than the ocean. Hundreds of hands throw flowers and turmeric rice at you. You're close to the throne now … oh, what is this! Adada! Who is this who shows up like an obstacle to all the good omens? There is a woman there, her hair loose, standing between you and the throne. "No, don't!" she says, and stops you from sitting on the throne. You push her aside. Adada! … What is this, now? Why is the smoke clouding everything? I can't see a thing!'

'Look, look! Look carefully! See through the smoke and tell me, what happens next?'

'Ilavarase! Please forgive me. There is too much smoke. I can't see a thing!'

'But look, appane, look hard! Who is that woman? See if you can get a good look at her face, at least! Have you seen her before?'

'Ilavarase! That woman has disappeared, as have you. The sabha, the throne, the crown have all disappeared. Someone with magical powers is in the palace right now! It seems someone has deliberately made smoke appear and cloud my vision ... Oh! Oh! Oh! Aiyo! My face is on fire!' Vandiyadevan cried, and raised his hands to his face. He trembled for a while, and then opened his eyes.

He could see every nerve in Madurantaka Devar's body strain against his muscles. The prince's face was aflame with rage, his eyes like a blazing furnace.

Vandiyadevan felt a little frightened by this sight. He wondered if he had kindled the prince's desires too much and overplayed his hand.

'Look again! Look and tell me what you see!' Madurantakar said.

'Ilavarase! There is no point now. A vision that vanishes will not reappear immediately. It will be some days before I can conjure it up again. If you would like me to, I can look at the flame and tell you whether any other vision appears.'

'Yes, yes, tell me! Whatever you can see, tell me!'

'The people are all scattered and confused. They are in grief and they are furious. A messenger has appeared and is giving them some news. Someone from the royal family has drowned at sea, he says ... Aiyo!

The poor man! The people are going to beat up the messenger. Ilavarase! If something of this sort happens, please don't make an appearance and walk among the people. Even if you must, please do be careful!'

'Did the messenger not say who it was that drowned at sea?'

'I couldn't hear his words clearly through all the commotion and noise. That vision has disappeared now. Now, I see a terrifying crowd before me, men wearing necklaces of skulls bones! Oh, no, these are the Kalamukhas! One among them wields a sword so large, it is taller than he is! Before him is a sacrificial slab ... Ilavarase! A prince has appeared now. The Kalamukhas surround him and start chanting. Aiyo! Don't ever, ever allow yourself to go anywhere near a crowd like this!'

Madurantakar broke into a sweat. His body began to quake.

Vandiyadevan noticed this and said, 'Ilavarase! I'm not able to make out anything else. Please forgive me. I feel dizzy. My vision is blurring. I'm blacking out ... someone has cast a spell on me! I will have to meet you elsewhere, at another time, and tell you everything.'

With this, he held his head in his hands.

At that moment, a palace servant appeared and announced that Sembiyan Mahadevi had ordered him to escort the prince to her.

Madurantakar determined to pour out all his anger and frustration on his mother as he left.

'Aiya! I'm not able to bear this headache. Please permit me to step outside the palace and get some air,' Vandiyadevan said.

~*~

The life of the Pazhaiyarai royal physician's son Pinagapani Pandidan had taken an unexpected turn. Until a few days ago, he had been happy to learn the science of healing from his father. He had had no other ambition than to follow in the physician's footsteps. But on their way to Kodikkarai, Vandiyadevan had filled his head with all manner of things. He had told him much about the world that Pinagapani had not known. And Vandiyadevan had not stopped there. People in the first blush of love feel compelled to talk about it to someone or the other. Vandiyadevan could see that the physician's son was something of a moron, and felt it was safe to say things to him and trust that he would not put two and two together. Vandiyadevan had spoken of the dangers of allowing a woman into his heart. He had told Pinagapani of having met the love of his life, and of the agony and ecstasy this had stirred in him.

Pinagapani felt little interest in this at first. But as Vandiyadevan waxed poetic about his lady love, curiosity got the better of Pinagapani, as did jealousy and frustration. He asked Vandiyadevan what the woman's name was, and where she was from.

The latter refused to tell him. This further angered Pinagapani. By the time they reached Kodikkarai, he had decided Vandiyadevan was the enemy.

The embers that Vandiyadevan had lit in his heart sprang into flame once Pinagapani saw Poonguzhali. But she not only rejected his proposal, she also mocked him. When he saw that she treated Vandiyadevan differently, as if he was entitled to more respect from her, Pinagapani was driven mad. He found Pazhuvettaraiyar's men and told on Vandiyadevan.

But the men failed to capture Vandiyadevan, and so arrested Pinagapani, who was then imprisoned in the Pazhuvettaraiyars' dungeon. This made him even more furious with Vandiyadevan.

We already know that he had been released before Kundavai Piraatti could have him let out of prison. It was the Pazhuvoor Ilaiya Rani who had freed him. She had her reasons. She had felt angry and betrayed by Vandiyadevan for sneaking out of the palace. When she'd learnt that he had gone to Pazhaiyarai and then Lanka, she began to grow suspicious about him and his motives. She knew that he would have to come back to Pazhaiyarai someday, to report to Kundavai Devi. She had to find someone trustworthy in that city, to let her know the moment Vandiyadevan returned.

It struck her when she spoke to Pinagapani that he was the ideal candidate, and gave him this tremendous responsibility.

'The man who betrayed you will return to Pazhaiyarai sometime soon. Keep your eyes peeled for him. As soon as he shows up, make sure you find out where he goes and what he does. You must send word to me right away. You will be suitably rewarded.'

On top of this, Chinna Pazhuvettaraiyar had sent for him too.

'If you alert us the moment that traitor returns so we're able to catch him, I will absorb you into our army of spies, and make you one of the most powerful generals,' Chinna Pazhuvettaraiyar promised him.

With this, Pinagapani lost all interest in the medical profession.

Now, as he roamed the streets of Pazhaiyarai, keeping an eye out for Vandiyadevan, he built castles in the air, seeing himself as a general in Chinna Pazhuvettaraiyar's army, and rich with the rewards the Pazhuvoor Ilaiya Rani would bestow upon him.

Every now and again, he would believe he had found him. He would run up to random men on the street, stare into their faces and then cry, 'No, not he!' He would mumble these words over and over to himself, even as he walked away. The residents of the city had come to believe he had lost his mind.

Even so, Pinagapani did not let up. He took his mission seriously. When Madurantakar and his entourage entered the palace, Pinagapani did not pay them much mind. It hadn't occurred to him that Vandiyadevan might be in their midst. He focused instead on the other procession, the one led by Tirunaaraiyur Nambi. He went round and round, staring at the faces in that procession. On one such round, he saw the procession of Madurantakar making for the palace gate. He caught sight of a man on a horse by Madurantaka Devar's side. A sudden doubt crept into his mind. But the man disappeared into the palace before Pinagapani could get a good look.

19

SAMAYA SANJEEVI

Pinagapani was not able to work his way into the sabha when Nambiyaandar Nambi[1] was being honoured there. He found himself at the periphery of the crowd, which had spilled out beyond the threshold, and had to peer inside to see what was going on. We already know that Vandiyadevan had eyes only for one face. Pinagapani, for his part, had eyes only for Vandiyadevan's face. And observing all this silently, without seeming involved in the proceedings in any way, was yet another man. He is none other than our old friend Azhvarkadiyaan.

After the sabha had dispersed and Vandiyadevan had wrecked Madurantakar's peace of mind by telling him of his visions, our hero stepped outside the palace.

Pinagapani, who was standing nearby, went up to him and said, 'Appane! Who are you?'

Vandiyadevan looked at him with a start. But trying his best to cover it up, he asked, 'What did you say?'

'I asked who you were.'

'You asked who I was? But which "I" are you referring to? This body which is made up of the Panchabhootams, the five elements—earth, water, wind, fire and space? Or the soul that lends life to this body? Or the Paramatma, the god from whom all souls emerge and to whom all souls return? Appane! What sort of question have you posed? There is no you, and there is no I. All we have is the grace of God, who created this illusory world and all the illusions it contains. Your doubts about pashu, pati, paasam—animals, the lord, emotions—can only be cleared by enlightened beings like Tirunaaraiyur Nambi, so go ask him!' Vandiyadevan said, and then rushed to his horse, which was standing at the entrance to the palace. He leapt onto the animal, and made off at a gallop. After some time, he realised Pinagapani had no intention of pursuing him and slowed down his horse.

But the physician's son was not quite that easy to fool, was he? His suspicions had just been confirmed. He went to the chief of the city's security detail, and told him he had spotted the spy. He accompanied the two guards the chief sent and did a round of the city. Just as he had expected, they didn't have to wait long to meet Vandiyadevan.

When Pinagapani saw him coming down the road, he cried, 'That man is the spy! Arrest him!'

'What happened to you, appane? Have you gone mad?' Vandiyadevan said.

'Whom are you referring to as "mad"? This body made of five elements? Or the soul? Or the Paramatma? Or pashu-pati-paasam?'

'Your incoherent babbling makes it evident you're a lunatic.'

'Oh, I'm not a lunatic! I'm the physician who accompanied you to Kodikkarai! Guards! This man is the one who escaped from Thanjavur and ran to Lanka, the spy for whom a search is on! Arrest him right away!'

The guards went up to Vandiyadevan.

'Careful! Don't listen to this man, you'll be making a huge mistake! I am the nimithakaaran who has come here at Prince Madurantaka Devar's behest!' Vandiyadevan said.

'No, no! This man is a liar! Arrest him right away!' Pinagapani shouted at the top of his voice.

By this time, a crowd had gathered around them. Some were inclined to believe Vandiyadevan and spoke up in support of him; others took Pinagapani's side.

'This man doesn't look like a nimithakaaran,' one said.

'He doesn't look like a spy either,' another said.

'Can a nimithakaaran be quite so young?'

'Why not? Will a spy head out in the open on a horse?'

'Why would a nimithakaaran carry a sword?'

'If he's a spy, whose spy is he? And what is he doing in Pazhaiyarai of all places?'

In the middle of all this, Pinagapani cried again, 'Arrest him! Arrest him right away! Those are Pazhuvettaraiyar's orders!'

The moment they heard the name 'Pazhuvettaraiyar', most of the people began to sympathise with Vandiyadevan. They thought hard to figure out how they could help him escape from the Pazhuvoor king's clutches.

In the meantime, Azhvarkadiyaan had made his way to the crowd.

Suddenly, he hollered, 'Is the nimithakaaran who accompanied the prince here?'

'He is a spy!' Pinagapani cried.

'What nonsense! If the nimithakaaran who came here with Madurantaka Devar is here, step forward! The princess has asked you to come to her,' Azhvarkadiyaan said.

Vandiyadevan's heart leapt. 'I'm the nimithakaaran!' he said, joyfully. 'Here I am!'

'Don't let him go! Don't let the spy escape!' Pinagapani shouted.

'If you're a nimithakaaran, prove it! Once you do, you may accompany me to the princess,' Azhvarkadiyaan said, with a quick wink at Vandiyadevan.

'How would you like me to prove it?' Vandiyadevan asked.

'Do you see those two horses running towards us? It appears the horsemen are rushing here with some important news. If you're a nimithakaaran, you should be able to tell us what news they bring.'

Vandiyadevan stared at the men on horseback and said, 'Of course I can tell you. The men are coming here with the news that a member of the royal family has had an accident ... it has something to do with water. They are bringing this terrible news to us.'

He had barely spoken the words when the horses were upon them. The people blocked the horsemen's path, and so they had no choice but to halt.

'You appear to be messengers. What news do you bring?' Azhvarkadiyaan asked.

'Yes, we are messengers. We bring terrible news. Prince Arulmozhi Varmar's ship was caught in the storm at sea. The prince jumped off the ship to save someone and drowned!'

No sooner had the messenger spoken than screams of 'Aiyo! Aiyo!' began to rise from the gathering.

In no time at all, the crowd had grown tenfold. Men and women and children and old people and youngsters milled about. Some wept, some beat their breasts and some fired questions at the messengers.

Most people of the city knew that the Pazhuvettaraiyar brothers had something against Prince Arulmozhi Varmar. It was also rumoured that they had sent a ship to Lanka to arrest the beloved prince. So, many began to mutter about the brothers. Soon enough, they started cursing them out loud.

'The Pazhuvettaraiyar brothers must have conspired to drown the prince!' some said.

Their accusations and wails and curses were louder than the waves that had crashed into those shores a couple of days earlier.

The messengers were not able to proceed to the palace. They tried to get the crowd to give way, but no one would relent. People threw questions at them:

'When?'

'Where?'

'How?'

'Is this confirmed?'

'Why are you simply standing here? Go on, part the crowd and escort the messengers to the palace!' Azhvarkadiyaan said to the guards.

The two guards had been stunned by the news. At his urging, they snapped back to life and began to push people aside to make way for the horsemen. The messengers slowly made some headway, even as the crowd surged and closed in behind them, following them to the palace.

And in that crowd, of which every constituent member was mourning the prince and lamenting the news, a lone voice shouted, 'Aiyo! This is a conspiracy! They have conspired to help the spy escape!'

No one cared for the physician's son and his panicked cries. They didn't even hear him. They could only think of the prince and the disaster that had befallen him. And just as a flood in a great river sweeps a little twig away with it, the crowd swept up Pinagapani and carried him along.

Vandiyadevan had got off his horse even as the crowd had begun to gather. Now, as they surged towards the palace, Azhvarkadiyaan went to his side and held him by the arm. 'Leave the horse and come with me! You can always find the horse later,' he whispered into Vandiyadevan's ear.

'Appane! You're a Samaya Sanjeevi![2] If not for your showing up in the nick of time, who knows what would have happened to me!' Vandiyadevan said.

'But you've made a career of this, haven't you? Get into some sort of scrape, and have someone rescue you in the nick of time!'

The two men then stepped to the side of the road so they wouldn't be swept up into the crowd. Once the gathering had moved some distance away, Azhvarkadiyaan led Vandiyadevan in a different direction. They went to the same locked house we've encountered before, in the street where the palaces were. They entered the garden and walked in the shadow of the trees lining the river. Soon, they came to a clearing with a view of the water. A boat waited in the water, and a woman was sitting in the boat.

The moment he saw her, Vandiyadevan's heart jumped to his throat.

20

MOTHER AND SON

When the servant arrived with the message that his mother had sent for him, Madurantakan made his way to Sembiyan Mahadevi.

The entire empire admired Periya Piraatti for her limitless piety and devotion to Shiva. Not so long ago, her son, too, had seen her as divinity. Now, all the adulation he had felt for his mother had transformed into anger and abhorrence.

A mother who had betrayed her own son and sided with the usurpers of his throne could not be found even in mythology and folklore, he thought. What had he done to be born of such a woman? All the love he felt for her turned into disgust, day after day, as the same thoughts ran incessantly through his mind. How could a mother do this to her own son?

He had worked himself up into a rage on the way, but when he saw his mother, whose face was the very picture of peace, some of his anger abated.

He followed custom and bowed to her. She blessed him with, 'May your store of Shiva bhakti, the greatest treasure one could have, grow!' and led him to a chair.

The words hit him like an arrow in the chest. He bore it in silence.

'Madurantaka! Is my daughter-in-law well? Is everyone in your father-in-law's and the Dhanadhikari's family well?' his mother asked.

'Everyone is well,' her son said, and then mumbled, 'Why do you care, anyway?'

'Did you meet the emperor before you left Thanjavur? How is his health?'

'I met him to take my leave. His health deteriorates by the day. His mind is even more troubled than his body,' Madurantakan said.

'What do you mean, my child? What has happened to trouble him so much?'

'People who have committed crimes, who are the perpetrators of injustice, who have snatched away what rightly belongs to someone else so they may enjoy it ... is it not natural that they are troubled?'

'What do you mean? Of what crime or injustice is the emperor guilty?'

'Isn't it enough that he has occupied the throne on which I should rightly sit, for so many years? Is that not a crime? Is that not injustice?'

'My child! How has your heart, which was pure as milk, begun to churn such poison? Who has instigated you to think such evil thoughts?' his mother asked with great compassion.

'No one has instigated me. Why do think your son is such a simpleton as to be led astray by someone else? Do you believe I am incapable of independent thought?'

'However intelligent one might be, one's heart and mind remain vulnerable to instigation and manipulation. They say even a stone can turn to powder if the right tools are used. Wasn't Kaikeyi led astray by Manthara?[1]'

'I am all too aware that women's hearts and minds are vulnerable to instigation!'

'Madurantaka! To whom are you referring?'

'Thaaye! Why did you send for me? Will you please tell me?'

'You were present at the sabha, were you not?'

'Yes, I was. You sent a palanquin to bring a mendicant boy to the palace, seated him on the throne and made a great fuss over him. He must be so filled with arrogance by now that he wouldn't be able to tell his foot from his head!'

'Aiyo! Please don't blaspheme like this, my son! The esteemed personage who graced our sabha might be young, but he has been blessed by Lord Shiva himself. He is steeped in knowledge of the ...'

'He might be a great personage, and my thinking less of him will not reduce his greatness, will it? I have not objected to your paying obeisance to this esteemed personage either. Now, will you please tell me why you sent for me?'

Sembiyan Mahadevi heaved a weary sigh. Then, she said, 'I'm stunned by the change I see in your behaviour, in your very nature. I didn't think in my wildest dreams that a couple of years in Pazhuvettaraiyar's palace would cause such a transformation in you. Well, whatever it is, I must do my duty. I must fulfil the promise I made your father. Or, I must try for as long as I can to make it come true. Before I tell you the reason I sent for you, I must tell you my story ... the story of how I met and married your father. You must listen patiently.'

Madurantakar leaned back in his seat, and rested his arms on the sides of the chair as a sign to his mother that he was all ears.

'You have visited my birthplace Mazhapadi a couple of times as a child. You have seen the Shiva temple there too. They say this was one of the temples commissioned by Kochengat Chozhan.[2] Your grandfather, my father, was an influential man from a prestigious family. Our clan is of an ancient lineage. Once upon a time, the Mazhavarayars were suzerain kings of great importance. During the war that was fought in Vijayalaya Chozhar's time, our ancestors entered into an alliance with the Pandiyas. And when the Chozhas won that war, the power of our clan was drastically reduced. I was told all these stories as a little girl, but this loss of glory never bothered me. My heart belonged to the Nataraja in the Mazhapadi temple.

'I'd heard of an incident in the history of Mazhapadi. An elderly gentleman told me about it when I was a child. Once upon a time, Sundaramurty Swamigal was passing through our town along with his disciples. There were clusters upon clusters of konnai trees around the temple, which completely hid the temple from sight. And so Sundaramurty passed by the temple without noticing it. He suddenly heard a voice saying, "Sundaram, have you forgotten me?" He swung round and asked his disciples, "Did any of you say anything?" The disciples had not heard a thing and no one had spoken either. Sundarar looked around for a temple, perhaps hidden, in the vicinity. He eventually found the temple behind the konnai trees, ran to the deity and sang the padigam which goes "Ponnaar Meniyane!"[3] Ever since, the lines *"Minne maamaniye! Mazhapaadiyen Maanikkame! Annai unnaiallaal ini yaarai ninaikkene!— He who shines like the most precious diamond, He who glows like a ruby in Mazhapadi, If not for he, who is my mother, Whom could I think of?"* have been indelibly etched into my heart. I used to go to the temple every so often. I would recite these lines before the statue of Nataraja.

'Over the years, the deity became the sole occupant of my heart. I dreamt that I would marry Shiva Peruman himself. I would imagine myself as Uma and Parvati and Dakshayani. I would try to emulate the meditation and austerities which had won them

Shiva Peruman for a husband. I would close my eyes and meditate. If anyone brought up the subject of my marriage, I would seethe with rage. As I transitioned from childhood to womanhood, devotion to Lord Shiva took root in my heart more than ever before. Everyone thought I was mad, those in my family as well as the townsfolk. But none of it mattered to me. I would only go home to eat and sleep. The rest of my time, I would spend at the temple.

'I would pluck flowers for the puja, make various kinds of garlands, adorn the deity with them and drink in the beautiful sight. I would often close my eyes and meditate. On one such occasion, I heard voices inside the temple. When I opened my eyes, I saw five or six men standing before me. The man who stood a little ahead of the rest was the one who captured my eyes and attention. It struck me that Shiva Peruman, on whom I had been meditating, had arrived with an entourage to claim me for his bride. I stood up and bowed before him. Tears were streaming from my eyes.

'He must have noticed this. I heard a voice ask, "Who is this girl? Why is she crying?" And my father's voice answered, "She is my daughter. It is as if she has traded her childhood for dotage ... she has been immersing herself in the worship of Shiva practically since her infancy. She comes to this temple and meditates and sings and sobs." When I looked up again, I realised that the gentleman before me was not

Shiva Peruman, but someone from a royal family. I was beside myself with humiliation. I took off as fast as I could, my only thought to run away from all of them. But the man who had enthralled me did not leave it there. He accompanied my father to our very house. My son, he was none other than my husband and your father, Kandaraditya Devar!'

At this, Periya Piraatti paused for a while. Reliving old memories had stirred emotions in her that she was not quite able to contain. Tears spilled out of her eyes again. She wiped them dry and then said, 'I then learnt that your father had recently been crowned the emperor of Chozha Naadu. His first act as the emperor had been to tour various Shiva temples in the land. He had crossed forty years of age by then. The wife of his youth had passed away. He had no intention of remarrying. But when he saw me, he had a change of heart. He asked me for my consent in my father's presence. When I saw him then, it struck me again that Shiva Peruman had come to marry me. I told him I would be most honoured to be his wife. We were married soon after, and your grandfather's title of "Mazhavarayar" was restored to him, as was the influence our clan had once wielded.

'My son! After our wedding, your father and I spoke at length and made a decision. We decided that our lives would be dedicated to the worship of Lord Shiva and to the well-being of his devotees. We decided that royal life was not for us. There was another crucial reason for this. My son! I didn't ever imagine that circumstances would necessitate my telling you all this. But I have no choice now and am compelled to tell you. Please listen to me carefully.'

With this, Sembiyan Mahadevi took a deep breath.

Madurantakan, for his part, listened with more interest than before.

21

'YOU CALL YOURSELF A MOTHER?'

Sembiyan Mahadevi, her eyes hazy with memory and devotion, said:

'My son! Your father Kandaraditya Devar ascended the throne under fraught circumstances for the empire. You're aware of the greatness of your grandfather Parantaka Chakravarti. Under his rule, the Chozha empire extended to Eezham in the south and the Krishna river in the north. But towards the end of Parantaka Chozhar's life, some terrible things happened to the family and the empire. The armies from Rettai Mandalam arrived like the legendary army of Ravaneswaran[1]. Your uncle, the eldest son of Parantaka Chozhar, Rajaditya Devar, went to fight this army. Takkolam saw a battle that could have rivalled the battle of Kurukshetra in intensity. The Rettai Mandalam armies were decimated, but your uncle lost his life on the battlefield.

'Parantaka Chakravarti's second son Arinjayar[2], too, had been badly wounded in the battle. But the soldiers were not able to find him, and no one knew whether he was even alive. Arinjaya Devar's eldest son Sundara Chozhar had gone to fight the war in Eezham when he was barely out of adolescence. There was no news of him either. The only Chozha scion who was by Parantakar's side at the time was your father.

'But your father had distanced himself from matters of the state even in his youth. He had immersed himself in the worship of Lord Shiva. He despised war. He thought it was bizarre that people fought each other to death because kings desired more and more land. He argued with his father and brothers about this, and tried to convince them to cease their warmongering. He spent all his time learning from elders who had studied Shaivism, visiting various sthalams and praying. He did not even desire to touch the sword and spear and other weapons. He did not study the art of waging war, or any of the allied disciplines. He believed ruling a kingdom necessitated lies and deception and betrayal and disguise and conspiracy and counter-conspiracy, to say nothing of abhorrent deeds like murder and plunder. "What is the difference between a thief who desires the belongings of others and a king who wants to invade another sovereign state?" he would ask.

'My son, destiny decided to weigh down your father with the burden of Chozha Naadu, even when he was revolted by everything to do with empire.

Parantaka Chakravarti, in his old age, was enfeebled by the loss of his beloved eldest son and the various threats that the empire was facing. He could no longer carry out the daily duties of a monarch, and delegated them to your father. The only reason your father accepted this was that he did not want to cause further distress to your grandfather, who appeared to be on his deathbed.

'The lady who had the good fortune to marry your father before me, Veeranarayani Devi, had already attained the feet of Lord Shiva. He was yet to meet me at the time. Your grandfather was sick with worry over who would take the reins of the kingdom after your father. By a stroke of luck, one of the search parties that had been sent out for Sundara Chozhar found him on an island off the Lankan coast, and brought him back.

'Parantaka Chakravarti had always been particularly fond of Sundara Chozhar. When your cousin was a baby, the emperor would often take him on his lap and play with him and coo to him, I believe. It had been predicted that this child would grow up to be a great warrior, and bring laurels upon the dynasty. This might have been among the reasons for your grandfather's adulation of him.

'And so, he stated that Sundara Chozhar should be made the crown prince, and that his progeny would become the future rulers of Chozha Naadu, after your father's time. That was destined to be Parantaka

Chakravarti's last wish, for he attained Shivaloka soon after. Your father was determined to fulfil it. He wanted to ensure that there would be no obstacle to Sundara Chozhar inheriting the throne after him, and to your cousin's descendants ruling the empire thereafter. He told me all this himself.

'Your father was a devout man, who had no desire to rule and no interest in the idea of empire. All he wanted to do was pray. And so, he delegated his royal duties to his brother Arinjayar and nephew Sundara Chozhar, and toured the temples of the land instead. As I told you earlier, he had no intention of remarrying at the time. And then, I happened to cross his path. It was my own devotion to Shiva, my madness as it was known, that made him ask for my hand. How lucky I was to have been blessed with such a husband as he! I must have spent entire lifetimes in prayer and austerities to deserve such good fortune.

'There are few mortals who have caught a glimpse of God. Very, very few. Shiva Peruman appeared as Rishabharoodar[3] before your father and escorted him to Heaven. Your father saw the lord as clearly as I see you now. You and I are obliged to fulfil the wishes of so great a man as he, my son ...'

As his mother trailed off, Madurantakar felt as if his heart was burning. His entire body shook with the effort of controlling his emotions. Finally, he said, 'How can you say that, thaaye? My father did not convey any of this to me. Why should I be obliged to do anything? In what way am I obligated to him?'

'My son! Listen! You were a toddler when your father attained the feet of Lord Shiva. And so, he was not able to convey anything directly to you. But he told me. Even when we married, we decided we should not have children. But, girl that I was, I found myself unable to resist having a child. The devotion I had felt for Lord Shiva now morphed into the love I felt for your father. My heart began to long for a child. My arms ached to hold a baby and clasp him to my chest and sing him lullabies and coo to him. When I saw other women holding or carrying infants, my body would yearn for it. My heart would feel as if it were on fire. I prayed to the lord I had worshipped all my life, and he in his generosity granted me that wish. He gave you to me. On the one hand, you made me complete. My heart and soul and body felt whole because of you. On the other hand, I was terrified your father would be angry with me. That good man was not angry with me. But before he left this world, he made me promise that I would keep his word for him.

'My son! I promised him that I would raise you to be indifferent to this earthly life of ours, and to understand that the only world that matters is the one that is yet to come, the abode of Shiva. I believed I had kept that promise until some time ago.

'But then, my son! My son, who is dearer to me than life itself, who is my everything, I have been hearing things of late. Things I never dreamt of. Things that make me shudder. Won't you tell me that all I have heard are lies, and reassure me that you are still the Shiva bhakt I raised, and soothe the hurt in my chest?' Sembiyan Mahadevi pleaded.

'Thaaye! Your words wound me. I don't understand to what you allude. What have you heard? And what do you want from me? What reassurance are you asking of me?' Madurantakan said, irritated.

'My child, you seem to have lost your ability to read my mind. You insist that I say it out loud. Fine, I will. I hear that your heart has found its way from the boundless Ganga that is Shiva bhakti to the little pond that is desire for a piece of earth. I hear that you wish to ascend the Chozha throne. I hear our enemies have sullied your thoughts. Tell me all this isn't true! Let my mind know peace and rest!'

Madurantakan rose to his feet.

Something in his mien made his mother stand up too.

'Our enemies have not sullied my mind. Are people who wish to see me ascend the throne that is my birthright "our enemies"? Are people who are willing to lay down their lives for me "our enemies"? No, never! Who is my true enemy, my greatest enemy? Why, the very woman who gave birth to me!' Madurantakan cried. 'It is you!'

He was so overcome with anger that he used word 'nee' rather than 'neengal', the informal singular rather than the respectful plural, to address his mother.

He forgot his father-in-law's instructions to appeal to his mother's empathy and sympathy, to win her over gradually and carefully. It was as if a dam had burst, and he couldn't stop himself from raging at her.

'Yes, you are my greatest enemy! No one else. You call yourself a mother? You call yourself a woman? Every mother does her utmost, gives her all, to ensure that her children get their due, that their rights are not denied them. Our stories and epics are full of such instances, and I have observed it in real life too. You alone stand against the order of a mother's nature! Are you truly a mortal woman, or a rakshashi in human disguise? What have I done to earn such betrayal? When have I ever let you down to prompt such treachery? Why are you so determined to tear from my hands what is rightfully mine, what belongs to me by every divine and human law, and give it to someone else?

'You claim this was my father's wish. You claim you made him a promise. Where is the evidence for all that? I don't believe a word of it. You claim someone has poisoned my mind. No, not at all! It is you whose mind has been poisoned! Someone has poisoned *your* mind and sullied *your* heart, and turned a mother into her own son's enemy! I will never give up my birthright! I will not step back from claiming the Chozha throne! Not even if you ask me to do so! Not even if my father returns from his resting place by Lord Shiva's feet and asks me to do so! This

Chozha empire is mine. The ancient throne is mine. The bejewelled crown that Karikaal Peruvalaththaan wore is mine. And I will claim them all. Here, I am wearing this rudraksha mala you gifted me. I've kept it on for all these years out of my respect for you. But it has only unmanned me and made me the laughing stock of the entire empire! I don't want it anymore. I will pull it off my neck right now, and you can do what you want with it!'

And having ranted like a madman, Madurantakan tried to remove the necklace of rudraksha beads from his neck. It wouldn't go over his head, and so he tried to tear it off. But the effort only hurt his skin. The rudraksha mala stayed intact.

Madurantakan was a handsome man, more good-looking than Sundara Chozhar's sons, whose appearance drew more from their bearing than their features. Madurantakan's face, with its enchanting features, possessed a soft, almost feminine, beauty that the two other princes lacked. Now, his fury and frustration had twisted that perfectly sculpted face. Unable to bear the sight, his mother closed her eyes.

She opened them again when he had subsided into silence. Her tone didn't change one bit as she spoke in the same calm voice she had used before her son's outburst, 'My son! Please be patient. Even if I am an evil rakshashi in your eyes, lend me your ears for a little while longer.'

Her unruffled manner rubbed off on Madurantakan, who said, 'I will listen to what you have to say. I didn't refuse to listen, did I?'

'You spoke of a mother's nature. Even an evil rakshashi will not betray her own child. Even wild animals try to protect their young from other wild animals. There is another reason I ask that you renounce your desire for the throne, aside from all that I have already told you. This desire will threaten your very safety, your very life. Is it so terrible for a woman to want the son whom she has birthed and raised to *live*? Is it a betrayal for a mother to want her child to stay alive? Your desire for the throne will instantly make you an enemy to Sundara Chozhar's sons. Aditya Karikalan and Arulmozhi Varman are trained warriors, veterans of several wars. You, on the other hand, have never held a weapon in your life! The entire Chozha army owes its allegiance to one or the other brother, having fought under their leadership. The generals will throw in their lot with them. And the princes have friends and allies in neighbouring kingdoms too. Who are your friends? Who are your allies? Whom do you have by your side, whom can you trust to stay by your side, if you go to war with them?

'My son! You know that the Dhoomaketu has been spotted in the sky for some time now. The entire world knows that when a shooting star appears, it bodes danger to a member of the royal family. All I want is that you not be the person in danger. My child, is it wrong for me to want my only son alive? Is this a betrayal to you?'

Her words softened her son's heart. 'Annaiye[4]! Please forgive me. If only you'd told me earlier that this was your cause for worry, I would have put your mind at rest in an instant. I am not without friends and allies. The most influential suzerain kings and most distinguished commanders in Chozha Naadu are on my side. The Pazhuvettaraiyar brothers stand with me, as does Kadambur Sambuvarayar. Your brother and my uncle, Mazhavarayar, is by my side. Neela Tangaraiyaar, Irattaikudai Rajaaliyaar, Kunrathur Perungizhaar have all thrown their strength behind me. They have promised to support me.'

'My son! I have no faith in their promises. They had once promised to serve Sundara Chozhar and his heirs, and now have no qualms reneging on that promise. Even if they were to be true to you, what support have they pledged? What are their miniscule armies to the vast one that Aditya Karikalan commands in the north or the equally large one that Kodumbalur Velaar leads in the south?'

'Thaaye! The kings who are on my side can bring me ten thousand men each at any time.'

'Well, let's leave the army aside for now. What about the people? Don't you know how much they adore the two sons of Sundara Chozhar? You saw it for yourself. If Arulmozhi Varman or Aditya Karikalan were visiting Pazhaiyarai, how the people would have thronged to catch a glimpse of them? There was a time when they had much affection for you. But your relationship with the Pazhuvettaraiyar brothers has lowered you in their esteem. Some even despise you.'

'Thaaye! I don't care for the love and adoration of the people. What use does it have for me? The people must be ruled. Whoever sits on the throne is their king and commander, and they must bow before him!'

'My son, the people who have been manipulating your mind have failed to instil in you even the most basic lesson a monarch must learn. No one can rule an empire for long unless he has the affection of the people. And no good will come of it either. What is the point of …?'

Even as Periya Piraatti was speaking, they were distracted by a great commotion at the palace gates. Wailing voices and angry curses and panicked questions rose from what sounded like thousands upon thousands of people, surging like a tidal wave and roaring like the stormy sea.

'My son! Some terrible danger lies in wait for the Chozha empire. These are only the first harbingers of this. I will make my way to the palace gates and find out what's going on. You stay right here,' Sembiyan Mahadevi said.

22

'DID YOU HEAR THAT?'

The moment he saw the boat, Vandiyadevan knew it was the princess who was seated inside. However, given that Azhvarkadiyaan stayed where he was, Vandiyadevan, too, hesitated to step forward.

'Appane! What are you lingering for? Ilaiya Piraatti has been waiting for you for a very long time. The moment you get on the boat, tell her the good news that the prince has reached Chozha Naadu and is safe. Don't waste time drawing out an account of your heroic deeds! I'm heading back now. We've unleashed a beast in Pazhaiyarai, the beast of riots. I'll go see whether this beast can be caged again. Look what trouble your adventures land us in!' Azhvarkadiyaan said, and then went back the way they had come.

Vandiyadevan looked after him in surprise. How did he know everything about everything? For all that, he hadn't asked Vandiyadevan a thing. Was it all from conjecture and deduction? Or did he truly know all that he appeared to? They said there were two kinds of mendicants—the religious ones who sought alms as a hereditary tradition, and those who sought alms because they were hungry. There were perhaps two kinds of spies too. Vandiyadevan had become a spy by necessity, and so he had a tendency to get into all sorts of scrapes. This Vaishnavite must be a spy by birth, carrying on the tradition of a grand lineage of spies, and so he went about his business calmly and quietly. But whom was he working for? And could one believe the life story he recounted?

Having reached the edge of the water by now, Vandiyadevan looked up at the princess's face. And, he forgot Azhvarkadiyaan. He forgot his mission. He forgot the world and he forgot himself.

This beloved face had never really left him. When he had been separated from it in person, he had seen it in his dreams, in the raging waters of the storm and through the gentle breeze of an evening. He saw it in hills and in valleys, in forest and ocean. And yet, how was she so much more beautiful in person than in all those visions? Why did his heart beat so fast? Why did his throat close up?

Vandiyadevan was barely conscious of what was going on as he waded through the water and climbed onto the boat. The princess gestured to the boatman, and the boat began to move. Vandiyadevan's heart felt as if it was swinging through air.

'Nimithakaara! Are your talents reserved for the prince? Or will you tell my future too? And how will you do it? Do you look at the alignment of planets and stars? Or do you study the movement of crows and sparrows? Perhaps the lines on one's palm? Ah, it appears you read faces. Why else would you be staring at my face like that? Be careful! If this is how you go about it, no highborn lady will invite you again to tell the future!'

The princess's voice poured into his ears like the gentle notes of a flute.

'Ammani! I was not looking at your face to tell your future. It struck me that I've seen this face before, sometime, somewhere. I was trying to recall the context.'

'I know, I know. You're absent-minded, of course. Let me remind you. It has been about forty days since you first saw me. It was at the house of the astrologer in Kudandai, and then you saw me the very same day by the shore of the Arisilaru.'

'Ammani! Stop this ... I'm not able to bring myself to believe you!' Vandiyadevan said. 'Has it been only forty days since I first saw you? Was it not forty thousand years ago? Have I not seen you a hundred thousand times in a hundred different births? Have I not seen you in the bowels of the earth and on the peaks of mountains? Have I not seen you at the edge of a pond at the very top of the world, and have I not seen you through the undergrowth of the densest forests on earth? Did I not save you from a tiger that was chasing you in that dense forest? And did I not throw a spear at the tiger to save you? In that birth, I was a hunter. I spread nets to catch beautiful birds of various colours and brought them to you. You took them from me and released them into the air right away, laughing as they soared back into the skies. In another birth, I was a fisherman. I went from river to river, pond to pond, ocean to ocean, I sailed the seas for faraway lands so I could find fish you had never seen before, and I would bring them to you, only for you to throw them back into the water and clap your hands as they danced and jumped from relief. I dived to the very bottoms of oceans for pearls and corals, and brought them back to you. You would hold them and sift them through your fingers and then call all the little boys and girls in town and distribute those hard-won gifts. I searched out the three-hundred-year-old ilanthai tree which yields a single fruit every thirty years, and brought it back for you. You gave it to your pet mynah and giggled as the little bird poked the fruit with its beak over and over again. I went to Devalokam itself and brought back mandara flowers, only for you to say, "How can these compete with the beauty and fragrance of the mullai flowers that grow in Chozha Naadu?" I asked Indra for the invaluable gemstone pendant he wears, and you said, "How will I so much as touch something worn by that filthy Indra?" I went to Kailash and begged Parvati Devi for her silambu[1] and brought those precious ornaments back for you. You said, "Aiyayo! How can the silambu that have graced the golden feet of Jaganmata be sullied by mine? What blasphemy! Go, give it back!" I went to battle and defeated the kings of all sixty-four empires, and brought back their crowns as an offering to you. You kicked them all away, and I was worried that your delicate feet would have been hurt from the force. Ilavarasi! Is this the truth? Or is it the truth that I saw you for the first time only forty days ago?'

And yet he was not finished. 'Devi! Something else comes to mind. Once, we got on a silver boat that had ivory oars with golden grips and we rowed it across the sky with its waves of moonbeams ...' he began.

'Aiyayo! This nimithakaaran seems to have gone completely mad! We'll have to turn the boat back and head for the shore!' the princess said.

'No, devi, no! I was completely fine until I saw the boat from the shore. How else could I have found a way to enter Pazhaiyarai? How else could I have convinced Madurantaka Devar I was a nimithakaaran and entered the palace? How else could I have tricked the physician's son? It was only after I got on this boat and saw your beautiful face that my brain has got as addled as a man who has had a drink too many!'

'Aiya, in that case, please refrain from looking at my face. Look at the clear waters of this lake instead. Or the blue sky, or the trees that graze the sky. Or the grand mansions of the city or the marble steps of the gardens, or the flowers that blossom alongside the lake, or the face of this deaf-mute boatman. And, as you look at all these, tell me what became of your mission. Was it a success or failure? Did you bring the prince back home? Is he well? Where have you left him, and in whose care? Tell me this first, and then you can tell me the entire story of all that unfolded since you first left these shores,' the princess said.

'Devi, if my mission had not been a success, would I have been able to come back here and show my face to you?' Vandiyadevan asked. 'I brought the prince back from Lanka. There were a thousand obstacles, and I brought him here overcoming all those. I cannot tell you whether he is well now. When I left him, he was burning with fever. But I have left him in safe hands. I've charged the boatwoman Poonguzhali and the young man who collects flowers for the temple puja Senthan Amudan with his care. They would lay down their lives a hundred times over to save the prince.'

At that very moment, a medley of screaming, confused, blathering voices, interspersed with wails and curses, rose from the direction of the palace. The princess and Vandiyadevan looked that way anxiously.

'Did you hear that? What is the commotion about? It sounds like an angry mob, doesn't it?'

'Yes. It does sound exactly like that,' Vandiyadevan said.

The story continues in
BOOK 6

INFANT EMPEROR

An Extract

'THE TIME IS NIGH!'

We've been here before, this pallipadai temple which had been built a century earlier and was now a ruin. This was the spot where Azhvarkadiyaan had hidden and eavesdropped on Ravidasan and his band of fellow conspirators. Now, we find ourselves here again, with Vandiyadevan and the rest.

They brought Vandiyadevan and his horse to a corner of the ruin.

'Appane! You stay right here until we call for you. Don't even dream of an escape. Nobody can enter or get out of this forest except for those who know it like we do. If you try, you'll die trying!' Ravidasan said.

'And even if I do find the way out, you'll cast one of your spells on me and kill me, won't you? You're a mantravadi, aren't you?' Vandiyadevan said, with a laugh.

'Laugh, laugh … laugh all you want,' Ravidasan said, and laughed too.

At that very moment, a jackal began to howl in the distance. Right after, an owl hooted. Vandiyadevan's hair stood on end. Not from the cold, but from the sense that this forest was so forbidding that even the breeze was hesitant to venture inside. Why, even the rain hadn't dared pour here. As they had passed through the undergrowth, he had been surprised by how dry it was. There were barely a few drops of rain on the odd shrub.

It was stuffy in there. Vandiyadevan's waistcloth had dried by the time they reached the pallipadai. Only the cloth scroll he'd secured in his waistband was still wet. He spread it out to dry on a rock, and then sat on another rock and leaned against the wall. A lone man stood guarding him.

The rest of the men stood some distance away in a clearing. A man brought an old throne from the pallipadai and placed it there.

They sat the child whom they addressed as 'Chakravarti' on this throne. They then put out all the flares but for two. The smoke from the doused flares spread in every direction.

'Why isn't the Rani here yet?' a man asked.

'She has to choose the right time, doesn't she? I have asked her to come during the second jaamam too. Until she does, someone sing songs in praise of the Vazhudi clan!' Soman Saambavan said.

Idumbankari produced an udukku drum, and began to tap it in time.

The Devaraalan began to sing.

Vandiyadevan saw and heard all this from where he sat. He knew that the 'Vazhudi clan' referred to the Pandiyas. The song sounded like some sort of lament. The beat of the udukku and the tune of the song made him rather sad. He was able to catch some of the lyrics and he gathered it was a song that recounted the war that had played out at that very spot a century earlier.

There had been a fierce three-day battle between Varaguna Pandiyan and Aparajita Pallavan. The Ganga king Prithvipati had arrived to aid the Pallava king, and had lost his life on the battlefield. The pallipadai that had been raised in his honour was the one that now served as the conspirators' den.

Prithvipati's martyrdom was also the death knell for the Pallavas. With their armies scattered, a Pandiya victory seemed certain. It was then that the Chozhas came to the aid of the Pallavas. At the vanguard was Vijayalaya Chozhan, the bearer of ninety-six scars. He was an old man who had lost the use of his legs, but was borne into the battlefield by four soldiers. In each hand, he wielded a mighty sword. As he let out a battle roar, he spun the swords into a blur. To those who watched him, it was as if he was spinning the discus of Vishnu. Everywhere he went, the Pandiya soldiers on either side of him fell as corpses to the ground.

The fleeing Pallava armies returned to the battlefield inspired by the Chozha emperor.

'Jana jana jana janaar!' Ten thousand swords shone in the gloaming of the evening sun!

'Dana dana dana danaar!' Ten thousand spears sparkled silver as they flew through the air!

The swords and spears clashed. A hundred thousand heads fell to the ground, and a hundred thousand headless bodies fell too.

'Ee ee ee ee,' the horses neighed as they fell dead.

'Plee plee plee plee,' elephants trumpeted as they fell dead.

It was a flood, not of water but blood, a red river carrying dead people and animals. Twenty thousand carrion birds flew overhead, turning the blue sky black. Thirty thousand jackals came howling to the battlefield.

'Aiyo! O! O!' fifty thousand voices rose in a wail.

'Don't let them go! Catch them! Chase them! Slay them! Slice them!' a hundred thousand men roared.

'Ad-dum! Ad-dum! Ad-dum!' ten thousand victory drums boomed.

'Ploo! Ploo! Ploo!' twenty thousand conches blew.

'Ha! Ha! Ha!' sixty thousand ghosts laughed.

Vandiyadevan woke with a start. He blinked and looked about himself. He realised he had dozed off, leaning against the wall of the pallipadai. In his half-sleep, he replayed the terrifying dream he'd had. Was it a dream? No! It must be images triggered by the song the Devaraalan was singing.

At that moment, the man was recounting the scene of the Pallava and Ganga armies fleeing before the might of the Pandiyas. His audience was laughing with glee, and it was the sound of this awful laughter that had morphed into the ghosts' mirth in Vandiyadevan's dream and woken him. All of a sudden, Idumbankaari stopped playing the drum. The Devaraalan's song faded into silence.

A flare was moving towards them from some distance away. In its light, they could see a palanquin approaching. The bearers set it down. The curtains of the palanquin parted. A woman stepped outside. Yes, she was indeed the Pazhuvoor Rani, Nandini.

Vandiyadevan had only ever seen her in silk and ornaments, glowing like the goddess Mohini. Now, she appeared with her long hair fallen loose, the picture of the avenging goddess Ugra Durga. Vandiyadevan's heart stopped. His entire body began to tremble.

As Nandini walked towards the gathering, her eyes were focused on the child sitting on the throne. The child, too, looked at her. Everyone else stared at them both.

The woman who had come running in search of the child in the ruin—the woman whom he had addressed as 'Amma'—stood behind the throne.

As Nandini neared the boy, she held out both arms.

The boy looked back and forth between her and the woman standing behind him.

'You are my mother, aren't you? Not her?' the boy asked.

'Yes, kanmani[1]!' the Pazhuvoor Rani said.

'Then why does she call herself my mother?'

'She is your foster mother, the mother who raised you.'

'Why didn't you raise me? Why didn't you keep me with you? Why is she hiding me in some mountain cave?'

'Kanmani! This is to fulfil your father's desires. To take revenge against his murderers!'

'Yes, I know that,' the boy said, and jumped off the throne.

Nandini gathered him in waiting her arms and kissed the top of his head. The boy hugged her tight, as if he wanted to make sure she never left him again.

But this did not last. Nandini forcibly freed herself from the little arms that held her, and seated the boy back on the throne.

She walked to the palanquin and reached inside. She pulled out the sword we have seen before, once in the blacksmith's hands and once in her own. She gestured to the palanquin bearers, who then carried the palanquin some distance away and sat down by it, hidden from view.

Nandini approached the throne again, and placed the sword so it rested on the throne's arms.

The boy stared at it in fascination and then said, 'May I hold it?'

'Have some patience, my kanmani!' Nandini said. Then, she looked at Ravidasan and the rest, squinting her eyes as she put a name to each face. 'There is no one here other than those who have sworn the oath, is there?'

'No, devi!' Ravidasan said.

Nandini turned to him.

'Senapati ...' she began, only to be interrupted by his laughter.

'The title amuses you today. Who knows what will happen this day, next month?'

'Devi! How long we have been waiting for that day, wondering when it will be?'

'Aiyo, we're a handful of warriors. Our Chakravarti is a child. The Chozha empire is enormous, with a strong army. If we had hurried our mission, we would have been ruined. It is our patience that had brought us to this position—our mission will be accomplished shortly, the time is nigh! Ravidasare! Is there anything you wish to say? Is there anything anyone else wishes to say?'

Ravidasan glanced at the faces of his men, all of whom seemed content in their silence.

'Devi, there is nothing we have to say. But you have to tell us what you mean by "the time is nigh". Where, how and through whom will our mission be accomplished? Do grace us with this information too!'

'Indeed. I have come here expressly to tell you this. That is why I asked all of you to gather here and wait. And I asked that our Chakravarti be brought here too.'

Everyone, including the child on the throne, was looking at Nandini's face.

'Some among you were in a hurry,' she said. 'Some of you suspected that I might have forgotten the oath we took. That suspicion is baseless. I have more reason than any of you to remember that oath. I have not forgotten it. I have spent every day and every night of the last three years thinking of nothing else. Nothing else but how to create the opportune circumstance and moment, how to trap whom and for what, in order to accomplish our mission, in order to fulfil our promise, in order to keep our oath. The circumstances are finally right. The moment is here. The suzerain kings and great warriors of Chozha Naadu have split into two factions. Pazhuvettaraiyar, Sambuvarayar and some others have decided Madurantakan must be crowned next king. Kodumbalur Boothi Vikrama Kesari and Tirukkovalur Malayaman are opposed to this. I hear that Boothi Vikrama Kesari is marching on Thanjai with the army of the Southern Front, while Malayaman is gathering his men too. Civil war could break out at any moment.'

'Devi! We hear that you're going to great pains to avert this civil war. We hear that there will be peace talks in Kadambur Sambuvarayar's palace.'

'Yes, it is true that I have made these arrangements. But do you not see why?'

'No, we don't. Rani! A woman's heart cannot be read even by Sarveshwara, according to the elders. How can we ordinary mortals read yours?'

'True, you cannot. Let me explain. If civil war were to break out before our mission is accomplished, the outcome is not predictable. Sundara Chozhan is still alive. That cunning Anbil Brahmarayan is around too. These two men will intervene and calm down both factions. Or, one faction will emerge victorious, in which case we will not be able to fulfil our promise. That is why I have organised these peace talks. We must see our task through before the civil war actually breaks out. Once we achieve our goal, there will be no end to this civil war. Not until both sides are decimated. Do you now see why I have initiated these peace talks?'

The faces of the men betrayed their surprise and excitement. They couldn't help murmuring among themselves how incredible the Pazhuvoor Rani's foresight was. Even Ravidasan couldn't help admiring her plan.

'Devi! We are stunned by your foresight. We have now understood why you've called for peace talks. But then, you said the time is nigh, that our mission will soon be accomplished. Who will put it into action? How? When?' he asked.

'That will happen alongside the peace talks. An invitation has been sent under this pretext to our main foe, to attend these talks at the Kadambur palace. He will be there without a doubt. And that is where we will fulfil our oath. O Veerapandiya Chakravarti's Abaththudavigal! The time is nigh for you to avenge the injustice! Today is Sanikizhamai[2], isn't it? By next Sanikizhamai, our oath will be realised!'

All twenty people gathered there let out a war cry. Some jumped for joy. Idumbankaari drummed twice on the udukku. This woke the sleeping owls and sent them scurrying towards the higher branches. Bats flapped their wings and flew past. Vandiyadevan's horse shook himself nervously.

Vandiyadevan, too, stood up.

All he could tell from the distance was that Nandini had said something that had excited the people she was addressing. He hadn't heard her words.

Ravidasan gestured for everyone to calm down.

'Devi! Your last words have given us immense joy! We cannot believe that we have but a week to go to kill our foe and avenge our emperor! But who will have the honour?'

'It is natural that all of us should compete for this honour. And it is to ensure that this decision is made without anyone feeling upset that I have asked for our Chakravarti, the son of Veerapandiyar, to be present. Veerapandiyar's sword, too, is here. Whomever this little child hands his father's sword to will be the one who must avenge Veerapandiyar. And everyone else must stand at the ready. If the person chosen by our Chakravarti is not able to accomplish the task, everyone else must step in. I will be inside the Kadambur palace. Idumbankaari will be among the palace guards. We will help the chosen one to enter the palace. Do I have everyone's consent for these arrangements?'

The men looked at the faces around them. It appeared everyone was happy with the arrangements.

Ravidasan stepped forward, and said, 'Your arrangements are acceptable to us all. But there's another important issue. Whoever is chosen as our instrument of revenge will have supreme command here. Everyone must follow the chosen one's orders. Until our Chakravarti comes of age, whoever takes revenge will be the regent, and his word will be law.'

Nandini's face broke into a smile.

'And this includes me, yes?' she asked.

'Yes, devi. No exceptions can be made,' Ravidasan said.

'Excellent. Do I have everyone's consent for Ravidasan's proposal?' Nandini asked everyone else.

The men looked around again. They appeared hesitant to reply. One got the sense that some among them were not happy with the proposal.

Soman Saambavan said, 'How is that fair? How can our devi, who has done everything to aid us, be subject to the common man's word?'

'Please don't worry on my account. The only reason I am alive is to avenge the terrible murder of Veerapandiya Chakravarti. Whoever takes revenge will have my gratitude and servitude forever and ever,' Nandini said.

Then, she turned to the child who had been listening to all this, with or without comprehension, and said, 'Kanmani! This sword was your father's. Lift it with your little hands and give it to whomever you like most in this gathering.'

Ravidasan took a further step forward and said, 'Chakravarti, look at each one of us carefully! Whoever strikes you as the bravest and most courageous among us, hand the sword of the Pandiya clan to him!'

The infant emperor looked at every face around him, from his perch on the throne.

Everyone stared back at him, barely able to contain the excitement and anticipation of the moment.

Every pair of eyes pleaded: 'Pick me! Pick me!'

Ravidasan alone stared with an authoritative expression. His eyes and face did not plead, so much as command: 'Hand it to me!'

The child took his time. He gave each man the once-over a few times before placing his hands under the sword. It took him some effort to lift it.

The excitement of the group reached its peak.

The child swung round to face Nandini.

'Amma! You're the one I like most in this gathering. It is you who must rule on my behalf until I grow up!' he said, and handed over the sword to her.

NOTES

1. KODIKKAPAI

1   There are various interpretations of the composite word 'Kallulimangan'—if it is split as 'kal', 'uli' and 'mangan', it could mean someone who is so devious and determined as to blunt the chisel that is used to carve stone. If it is split as 'kal', 'uri' and 'mangan' and we assume that 'uri' was colloquialised into 'uli', it could mean someone who is so adamant and oblivious to reason as to insist that one be able to peel a stone. The saying essentially means a man of this nature will ruin everything in his path.

2   The ancient name for Poompuhar.

3   The word 'Peruman' has the same meaning as the word 'Perumaal' which means 'god'. Here, it is used in the same way as one would say 'my lord'.

4. A WHISPERED EXCHANGE

1   Kewda or screw-pine

5. RAKKAMMAAL

1   A form of address for a priest.

6. POONGUZHALI'S PANIC

1 'Pen' is 'woman' and 'buddhi' is intelligence. This is a derogatory phrase suggesting that women are intellectually inferior to men.

2 The fact that the emperor of Chozha Naadu is referred to as 'Chozhan' rather than 'Chozhar' is a shocking instance of disrespect.

7. A SONG IN THE FOREST

1 Literally, 'son of aththai'—son of one's paternal aunt. Since it was common for cousins to marry, this is also often used as an address for one's husband.

2 A song by Sundaramurti, one of the three famous Shaivite devotees, along with Appar and Tirugnanasambandar.

3 I've retained the Tamil words because this is one of Kalki's puns. 'Sudu kaadu' means 'cremation ground', and 'kaadu' means 'forest'.

4 This is a song by Sundaramurti, in praise of the Shiva deity in Tiruvaroor, which can be split into 'Tiru' (blessed or divine or holy) and 'Aroor' (the name of the place). The idea of a woman growing so thin from pining for her beloved that her bangles slip off her wrist is often found in Sangam-era poetry.

5 Another of Sundaramurti's compositions.

6 This might be a song made up by Poonguzhali, for there does not seem to be any such poem by Sundaramurti. Here, 'Kodi' is short for 'Kodikkarai'.

7 A piece of cloth worn by men over their shoulders.

8 In the Tamil tradition, marriage between first cousins was, and remains in some sects and castes, permitted and even desired, when they are born of siblings

of opposite sexes. Vandiyadevan suggests here that
Senthan Amudan and Poonguzhali are betrothed.

8. 'AIYO! PISAASU!'

1   This is a mythological tree, a divine wish-fulfilling tree
that emerged during the churning of the ocean in the
Kurma avatar of Hindu mythology.

2   An ancient Tamil instrument, similar to the harp.
In fact, the Tamil name of Jaffna in present-day Sri
Lanka—Yazhpanam—derives from this.

3   A ghost, usually a woman, the Tamil word for
'pishaacha', the flesh-eating demons of Indian
mythology.

9. THREE PEOPLE IN A BOAT

1   A unit of measurement of time, in Tamil, roughly
equivalent to three hours.

10. THE CHOODAMANI VIHARAM

1   The town of Poompuhar, referenced in Sangam
literature of all three periods, appears to have been a
flourishing port city, which was destroyed in the fourth
century perhaps by a tsunami or soil erosion. The
remains of the city are still underwater. Archaeologists
who have studied these ruins have found evidence that
Kaveripattinam was once the capital of the Chozha
empire, and that its importance as a trade centre was
at its peak during the reign of Karikal Chozhan. This
last is gleaned from various texts of Sangam literature,
and cannot quite be dated. It appears there were two
emperors of the same name, a couple of centuries

apart, the range being from the first century BCE to the second century CE.

2   Sundaramurti's given name.

3   The region known as Kayavarohan, that is modern-day Karvan in Gujarat, is where Lakulisha, the Shaivite revivalist who is recognised as the preceptor—and sometimes founder—of the Pashupata doctrine, established one of the earliest Shaivite centres in the region. Scholars believe Karonam could be a corruption of one of three words—Kayavarohanam, Kaya Arohanam or Kayavirohanam. The first of these refers to a deity descending to the earth in the human form to offer a devotee salvation; the second to a devotee ascending to the heavens with his corporeal body intact; and the third to a devotee's status when he has done enough good deeds to ensure he has no further births.

4   It was the norm to ask the deity of the city to grant what the poet was essentially seeking from the ruler, in the song he would sing to this ruler, who was then obliged to meet these demands which were disguised as prayer.

5   Modern-day Kedah, a state in Malaysia.

6   Likely a reference to the dynasty's flag, which must have borne the emblem of a crocodile.

7   The word used for 'mendicant' in the Tamil version is 'iravalar', which usually refers to travelling priests or monks, who undertake long journeys to visit temples or spread their religion. It is usually used alongside 'puravalar', its antonym or complement, which refers to a philanthropist.

8   Land exempt from tax.

9   This word means, literally, 'teacher', but can be used to address any elder who is believed to be learned. It is a derivation of the Sanskrit 'acharya'.

10   The women in the monastic order.

12. 'THROW THEM IN THE FIRE!'

1   The Tamil corruption of 'Harish Chandra'—the legendary king who always told the truth, usually to his detriment.

2   The goddess of sleep.

3   An ancient unit of measurement. A twenty-four-hour day comprised ten jaamams, and so Vandiyadevan had been asleep for about five hours.

4   A respectful form of address, usually to someone elderly. It literally means, 'O older one!'

5   Women's eyes are often compared to fish in Tamil literature. Scholars suggest that this refers not simply to the shape, but the liveliness and twinkle in those eyes, because fish constantly jump about in the water, an expression of joy as interpreted by the Sangam-era poets.

13. THE POISONED POTION

1   This is an elaborate greeting, hilariously ironic in the current context. One rarely uses it except in the presence of a king or guru. The movements that a dance or traditional martial arts exponent performs as obeisance to the gods before beginning a performance tend to be called 'vandanam'.

2 'Arasi' and 'Rani' are used interchangeably.

14. FLYING HORSE

1 A sect of Shiva devotees, ascetics reputed to make human sacrifices, and walk around with human skulls as begging bowls.

2 Folk theatre that tells the story of Kannagi from the Tamil epic *Silappadikaaram*, usually the episode where Kannagi burns down the city of Madurai to avenge her husband Kovalan, who was sentenced to death for a theft he did not commit.

3 Another term for the Devaraattam that we saw at the Kadambur Palace, where a dancer goes into a trance and becomes an oracle.

4 The planet Venus.

15. THE KALAMUKHAS

1 This translates literally into 'Lord Emperor!'.

2 The word 'nimitham' means omen. A nimithakaaran could be a clairvoyant, or a reader of omens, or someone who is possessed by the spirit of a deity at times. I have chosen to retain the Tamil word here because it is used fairly frequently later in the text.

16. MADURANTAKA DEVAR

1 A padigam is a collection of ten songs. The Devaratirupadigam refers to discrete collections of ten verses. These are likely scrolls or metal plates containing written versions of the songs. Or, they could be songs that were only known to some people in particular places, in keeping with the oral tradition.

2   The *Tiruvisaippaa* is the ninth of the twelve canonical works in the Shaivite tradition. The first nine are Devarams composed by various devotees, the eighth is the *Tiruvaasagam*, the tenth the *Tirumantiram*, the eleventh is *Prabhandamalai* and the twelfth is the *Periyapuraanam*.

3   Sembiyan is one of the earliest ancestors of the Chozhas. There are two versions of the story, one that says he is a descendant of Sibi, who sliced off his own flesh to feed a bird of prey so that the bird wouldn't kill a pigeon that had sought his refuge, and another that says 'Sembiyan' is another name for Sibi himself.

17. TIRUNAARAIYUR NAMBI

1   This refers to an incident that occurred in Tirunaaraiyur Nambi's youth. His father would offer food to the Pillaiyar deity in the Tirunaaraiyur temple. Once, when he had to travel to another town, he asked his little son to make the offering in his stead. The boy offered the food and asked the deity to eat. When the deity remained still, the boy began to weep and begged Pillaiyar to eat. The sight apparently moved the stone (pun intended), and Pillaiyar made an appearance to eat the food himself. Word got around, and the Chozha emperor of the time sent several plates as offering to the temple, and stayed to watch the deity eat. But the deity did not come to life again. The boy Tirunaaraiyur Nambi was sent for, and when he sweetly asked the deity to eat, Pillaiyar is said to have obliged so his devotee would not be disbelieved about the first time. This earned Tirunaaraiyur Nambi his

epithet. The phrase 'Pollaa Pillaiyar' means 'Pillaiyar who has not been sculpted'. It is believed the deity was a swayambhu, a rock found in the shape of Pillaiyar and not man-made.

2   One of the epithets to refer to Tirugnanasambandar, who, along with Appar and Sundarar, was one of the best-known composers of the Devaram in praise of Shiva.

3   Angayarkanni is the Tamil form of 'Meenakshi'.

4   This is, naturally, figurative. The phrase is often used in Tamil to speak of someone very young, as if the person were a suckling. Although it sounds stilted in translation, I believe it is an interesting turn of phrase, that says something about the quirks of this culture, and I chose to retain the phrase in translation rather than say something more generic and perhaps less confusing.

5   The name of the Shiva deity in the Arthanaareeshwara form.

18. THE NIMITHAKAARAN

1   A ceremonial fan, technically a fly-whisk, but used chiefly by royalty. This is typically white and made of yak's hair.

19. SAMAYA SANJEEVI

1   Another name for Tirunaaraiyur Nambi.

2   This is likely a reference to the Sanjeevi herb being a lifesaver for Lakshmana, the brother of the mythological Indian god Rama, and brought just in the nick of time by Hanuman.

20. MOTHER AND SON

1   A reference to an incident in the *Ramayana*, in which Dasharatha's second wife Kaikeyi who was even fonder of Rama than she was of her own son Bharata, was instigated by Manthra into demanding that her biological son be named king in Rama's stead and that the latter be exiled to the forest.

2   A Chozha king who is believed to have ruled in the seventh century and is one of the sixty-three Nayanmars or Shaivite saints.

3   This padigam, along with the translation, has been rendered in full in Chapter 15 (*Pazhaiyarai*) of Book 1 of this series (*First Flood*).

21. 'YOU CALL YOURSELF A MOTHER?'

1   The name 'Ravaneswaran' is used to refer to the King of Lanka from the *Ramayana*, ordinarily known as Ravana, by those who prefer to think of him as a good and just king, a devotee of Shiva and a virtuoso player of the veena whose only flaws were jealousy and avarice. Sembiyan Mahadevi acknowledges Ravana's devotion to Shiva here.

2   This is one of several contradictions in Kalki Krishnamurthy's text. History has it that Arinjayar was the third son, after Kandaraditya Devar, but he mentions in the Tamil version that Arinjayar was the second son of Parantaka Chozhar.

3   A form of Shiva, mounted on his bull Nandi.

4   Another word for 'mother', a more formal and respectful one, often used to refer to goddesses.

AN EXTRACT FROM BOOK 6: INFANT EMPEROR

1   This term of endearment refers to the pupil of the eye; it is a term of enormous affection, and I chose to retain it over 'darling' or 'dear'.
2   The equivalent of Saturday in Tamil.

Also from ekadā

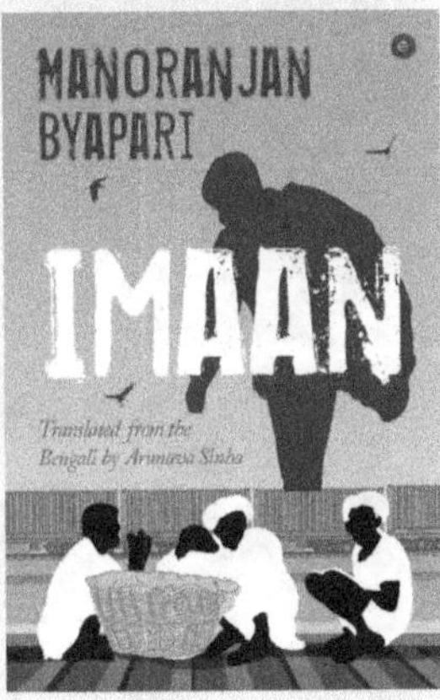

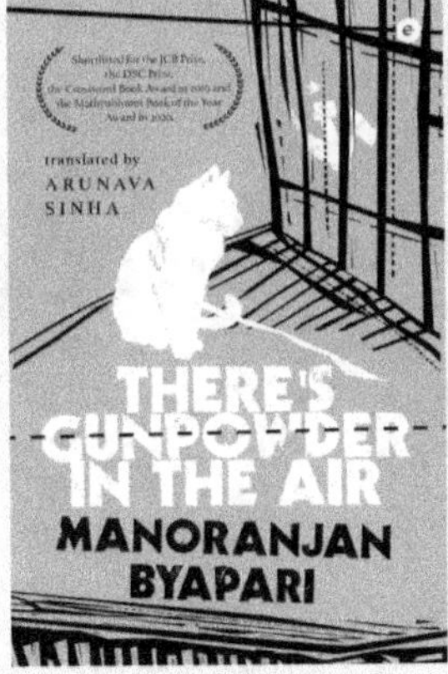

Also from ekadā

Also from ekadā

Also from ekadā

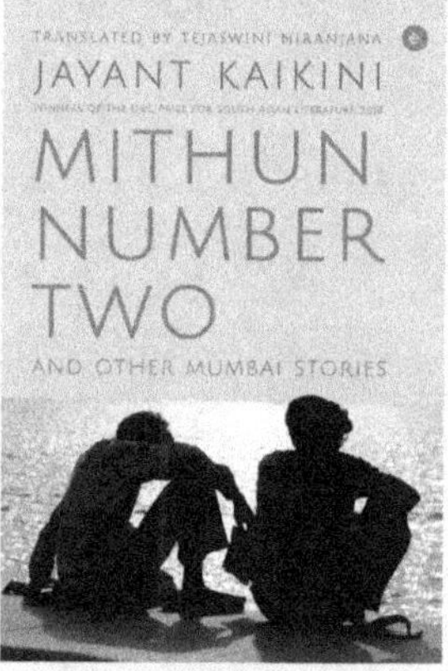

Also from ekadā

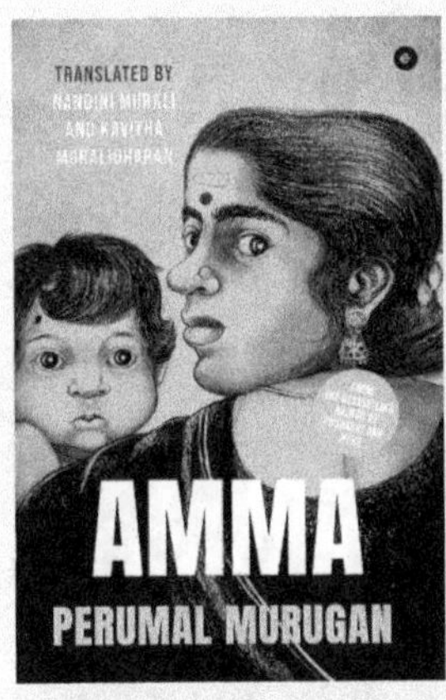

Also from ekadā

Also from ekadā

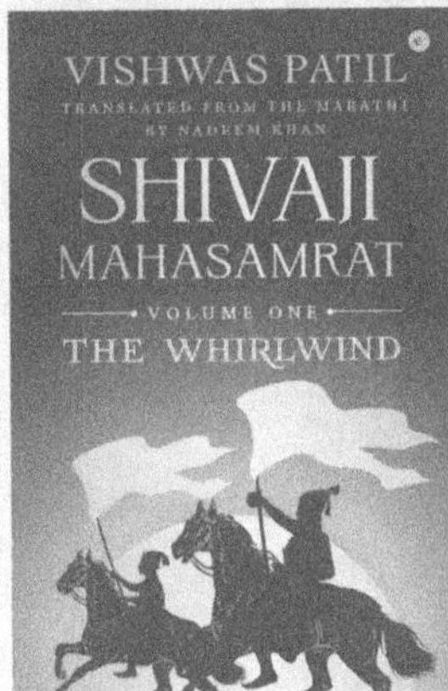

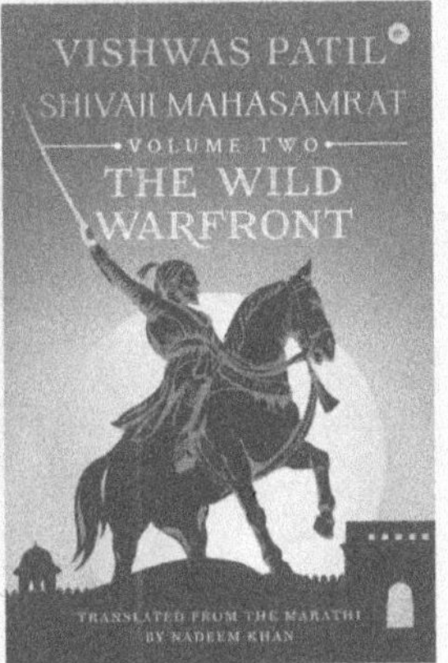

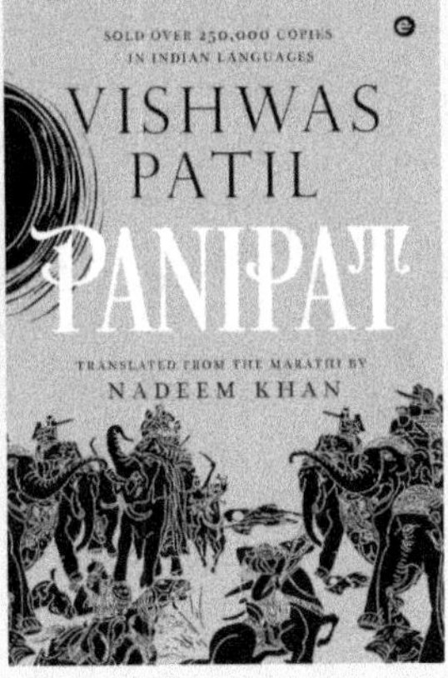